CW00969705

MATTHEW AN

Matthew and Sheila

Robin Jenkins

Polygon
Edinburgh

In memory of Colin

© Robin Jenkins, 1998

Polygon
22 George Square, Edinburgh

Typeset in Galliard by Hewer Text, Edinburgh,
and printed and bound in Great Britain by
Bell & Bain Ltd, Glasgow

A CIP record for this book is
available from the British Library

ISBN 0 7486 6239 1

The right of Robin Jenkins to be identified as author of
this work has been asserted in accordance with the
Copyright, Designs and Patents Act 1988.

The Publisher acknowledges subsidy from

THE SCOTTISH ARTS COUNCIL

towards the publication of this volume.

Part One

One

M atthew was nine when he discovered, or more accurately, decided, that he was one of the Chosen, those favourites of God who could no do wrong, or rather who, if they did what in others would be called wrong, were immediately absolved and protected from punishment. Appropriately it happened in a place so peaceful, spacious, and fragrant as to deserve the name heaven on earth: a machair or sea-meadow in the Western Isles, in summer. The fragrance rose from the myriad of tiny wild flowers. Small butterflies with wings as blue as the immense sky were also abundant: as were bumble bees humming happily among the bedstraw and larks ascendant singing for pure joy. Sheep and cattle grazed contentedly. Beyond sand dunes the Atlantic, blue, white, and green, came charging like great shining stallions up on to white sands, jockeyed by exultant angels. Like his grandfather, Matthew believed in angels, but, unlike his grandfather, he thought of them as beneficent and joyful. His grandfather spoke of them as wrathful and avenging.

The two of them were resting on a rock millions of years old, almost as old as God Himself. Matthew was dressed in white open-necked shirt and shorts, for it was warm and sunny. Grandfather was in his usual black, from hat to boots. A zealous little boy, Matthew, eager to learn, listened gravely as his grandfather complained aloud, in anguished mutters in Gaelic and English, that God had not been fair to him. A lifetime of preserving himself, his family, and his congregation from sinful world pleasures had not been rewarded as it should.

Matthew reflected that his aunts, and his mother, now grown up, were still not allowed to knit or cycle or even laugh on Sundays. His mother, the youngest, was also the most rebellious. That was why his grandfather had put a curse on her.

After a little cough, as if a fly had stuck in his throat, Matthew asked who these Chosen Ones were that his grandfather was talking about. He was greatly interested when his grandfather at length explained. He did not understand it all, but he found very attractive the idea of divine indemnity, for he was as fond of mischief as most boys his age and like them disliked being found out. He wasn't surprised that his grandfather had never been chosen, though he was a minister: he was always blaming God for something, and besides he was too old. The hymn said that it was children Jesus loved. Matthew himself was very eligible.

He carried out a test. At his feet a small green beetle crawled through the grass. It was enjoying itself in the sunshine. He put his foot on it and pressed hard. Then he waited. This wasn't the first time he had killed a creature that was doing him no harm, but on those former occasions he had felt guilty and fearful, half-expecting a voice from the sky to shout angrily at him. That had been because of his conscience. This time it was different. If you were one of the Chosen you wouldn't need a conscience. The sky was like a boundless bright smile. God wasn't displeased with him. He lifted his foot. The beetle lay still. Joy had gone out of it. It no longer glittered. It was dead.

His smirk of satisfaction soon turned uneasy. He had

forgotten the Devil. Didn't all crawlie things like beetles belong to the Devil?

His grandfather was always warning him about the Devil.

Cautiously, he asked: 'If I was one of the Chosen, could the Devil harm me?'

He was astonished by the vehemence of his grandfather's reaction. His grandfather looked as if he had swallowed not a fly but a big bumble bee and it was stinging his throat. He could scarcely speak. His eyes went skelly with horror and, which was more unusual, with pity.

'Miserable, unfortunate boy,' he mumbled. 'Do you not know that you are accursed? That the brand of the outcast is on your brow?'

No, Matthew didn't know that. What was on his brow was sunburn.

'From the day of your birth; nay, from the moment of your conception.'

Matthew had no idea what conception meant. Perhaps it had to do with his mother.

In any case his grandfather hadn't answered his question. He put it in another way. 'Is the Devil stronger than God?'

'Considering the evil that is in the world, evil triumphant, it would seem so.'

Considering too that the beetle had come alive again.

His grandfather rose. 'I must talk to you later. It is time you were told.'

Told what, Matthew wondered.

There were other children staying at the manse, Matthew's cousins, for the whole McLure tribe was present, to attend Aunt Morag's wedding. Only Matthew's father was absent. He had refused to come. 'And if you had any pride, Catriona, you wouldn't go either.' His father was an artist. He painted

5

ladies with no clothes on. He called Grandfather 'a vicious old bigot'. He didn't believe in God.

There was a glebe or large field attached to the manse. In it ministers in the past had kept cattle and sheep to augment their meagre stipends. It was surrounded by a drystone dyke to shelter it from the constant winds and from the rabbits that came loping up from the sand dunes for a change of diet. Grandfather grew vegetables, never flowers; these, he said, were useless. He was especially proud of his lettuce. So, on his way back to the manse, as he was considering what he could do to test God again, it occurred to Matthew that he could pee on the lettuce.

Amazed at his own daring, he crept to the corner where the lettuce grew and pee'd on them. What, he wondered, would happen now?

What happened was that he caught sight of his cousin, Ailie Spence, spying on him from an upstairs window. He was so startled that he wet himself. A notorious clype, she was sure to rush off and tell his grandfather and perhaps his mother too. She had already disappeared. Soon she would rush out and gleefully tell him how angry his grandfather was.

He was sorry if he had brought more trouble on his mother. She wasn't well.

He quite forgot that he was one of the Chosen.

When Ailie appeared she was alone. She ran towards him. In her blue dress she reminded him of the butterflies on the machair.

She came right up to him. He could have counted the freckles on her nose.

'I saw you, Matthew Sowglass,' she said.

'I wasn't doing anything.'

'Yes, you were. You were –' she hesitated: she lived in Bearsden, that very respectable suburb of Glasgow, where little girls were never rude – 'doing number one on Grandfather's lettuce. Look, it's still wet.'

'That's rain.'

'Don't tell lies. Grandfather will be awfully angry.'

'If you tell on me I'll tell on you.'

'Don't be silly. I've done nothing.'

That was true. She never did anything bad enough to be interesting. No one did.

'I saw you eating sweeties in church.'

'Everybody eats sweeties in church.'

Especially in Grandfather's church. His sermons lasted over an hour and were tedious.

'What will you give me if I don't tell?'

He had forty pence. He offered her twenty.

'I don't want your money. I've got four pounds. Tell you what, give me your compass.'

He was appalled. His silver-plated compass, given to him by his father, was his most cherished possession. With it in his hand he could imagine polar bears at the North Pole.

'I haven't got it with me.'

'Yes, you have. You always have. It's in your pocket.'

Gulls screamed overhead. He wished one would swoop down and peck out her tongue.

'Are you going to cry?' she asked, with false pity.

She should have known he never cried.

'Oh, never mind,' she said. 'I don't want your stupid compass, and I'm not going to tell. Do you know why?'

Yes, he knew. God would not let her.

'Because I hate lettuce and they make me eat it.'

That was one reason but there was another. God had made her change her mind. It was proof that Matthew was one of the Chosen.

Laughing, she skipped off towards the house, waving her arms as if they were wings. She was happy. He knew why. It was her reward for not telling.

Two

G randfather kept his promise or rather his threat to speak
to Matthew and tell him what he should have been told
years ago. He announced, portentously, that he wanted to see
Matthew in his study at half past seven.

All Matthew's cousins, the six of them, assumed that he was
going to be scolded sternly, though for what only Ailie knew
or thought she did. 'I didn't tell,' she whispered to Matthew,
'really I didn't.'

His mother took him for a short walk in the glebe. She
couldn't walk far, so they sat on a wooden bench. It had been
made by Grandfather. Grandfather had made much of the
furniture in the manse. As well as a successful grower of
vegetables he was a skilful carpenter.

'I was born here,' said Matthew's mother, 'in this beautiful
place.'

She was pale, breathless, and thin, but still beautiful and
determined.

'Your grandfather is going to tell you cruel lies.'

'Oh.' He was more interested than frightened.

'Did he say anything to you during your walk this afternoon?'

'He said I had the brand of an outcast on my brow. But it's
just sunburn, isn't it?'

'Yes, it's just sunburn.'

To his embarrassment she kissed him on the brow. He loved her, he liked her to kiss him, but not when people could see. He knew his cousins were watching.

'He said I was accursed from my conception. I didn't know what he meant.'

'Then I shall tell you.'

'You don't have to,' he said, anxiously, for he saw that she was close to tears. He saw too her resemblance to Grandfather.

'I must. I should have told you before but you were too young. You are still too young.'

'I'm nearly nine.'

'When you were born your father and I weren't married.'

That puzzled him but he let it pass.

'When we did get married it wasn't in a church. Your father objects to churches.'

He knew that. His father never went with them to St Cuthbert's in Lunderston, where they lived.

'For that reason your grandfather says you were born under a curse.'

'What does that mean?'

He asked out of politeness. He didn't care what it meant. Wasn't he one of the Chosen, with nothing to fear from anyone?

'It means that even if you live a life without sin or fault God will still reject you.'

'No, He won't,' he said, very confidently.

She had to smile.

'You see, Mum, I'm one of the Chosen. Grandfather isn't. That's why he's cross with me. He's jealous. He thinks God hasn't been fair to him.'

'How could God be well disposed to someone who puts a curse on an innocent child?'

'It doesn't matter whether I'm innocent or not.'

But she wasn't listening to him.

He took her hand. It was yellow and skinny, like a hen's. He remembered it when it had been white and warm.

'You know I'm not well, Matthew.'

'Yes. But you'll get better, won't you?'

'No, I will not. I shall be dead before the end of the year.'

He listened to a bird singing.

It was his custom when confronted by a situation too difficult to avoid it by thinking of something else. So he looked for the bird and found it among the rusty leaves of the stunted rowan. It was a yellowhammer, he thought.

'I've not been fair to you,' she said, 'or to your father.'

'It was your pain.'

Mrs Macdonald, the housekeeper, had told him that.

'Yes, it was my pain, partly, but I've been selfish and wilful.'

He couldn't bear to think what he would do if she died, but he knew his father would be heart-broken. In spite of their rows they loved each other.

She rose. 'You have an appointment to keep. But you don't have to go if you don't want to.'

'I want to. I'm not afraid.'

It would be another test.

Three

He was smiling when he knocked on the door of the study. After a minute or so his grandfather called, 'Come in.'

Ailie was there, with other cousins. She gave him a little push. 'You've to go in,' she whispered.

He opened the door and went in. He was surprised at how unafraid he was.

His grandfather was on his knees praying. Matthew noticed he was kneeling on a fat cushion, so that his knees wouldn't get hurt. He noticed too that there was a tiny green fragment on his grandfather's white beard, either a bit of lettuce or a caterpillar.

What, he wondered, was his grandfather praying for? If he thought God was displeased with him what was the use of praying? In any case God seldom gave people what they asked for. Matthew knew that from experience. He had learned that you had to help God by asking only for what you knew He could give you.

He waited politely for his grandfather to finish.

When his grandfather was getting to his feet, stiffly, Matthew offered to help him. His offer was refused.

The big black Bible was open on the desk. He hoped his grandfather wasn't going to read out of it. His grandfather always chose dull bits and went on too long.

The desk, though, was worth looking at. It had ships carved on it. His grandfather had made it many years ago.

Seated in a straight-backed uncomfortable chair his grandfather plucked at his beard and tried to look wise and good. Matthew thought he looked cunning and cruel.

'It is my duty,' said his grandfather solemnly, with a horrible grin, 'placed upon me by God, whose word is in that book, to tell you that you and your mother must leave this house tomorrow and never return. You have brought uncleanness into it.'

Well, Matthew didn't wash here as thoroughly as he did at home, but that was because there was so little hot water and so many people.

Today was Tuesday.

'We were going on Thursday anyway,' he said.

'They tell me that you are innocent, that the sin is not yours, but that book there contradicts them. They are wrong therefore. It would have been better for you if you had never been born.'

'Maybe it's you that's wrong, Grandfather.'

He didn't say it cheekily, but as a reasonable contribution to the discussion.

His grandfather was too astonished to be angry.

'I think it's because God didn't make you one of the Chosen. You told me that yourself.'

'This is the Devil speaking.'

'No, it's me, Matthew Sowglass. I'm one of the Chosen. I know that because when I killed a beetle on the machair I didn't feel bad. It became alive again. I thought it was the Devil did that but I think it must have been God.'

'Miserable boy, was it your mother who taught you to speak with such diabolical insolence?'

What did diabolical mean? When he got home he would look it up in the dictionary.

'She told me you would tell me cruel lies.'

It was then time to go.

His grandfather, he saw, wanted to be furiously angry with him, to call him terrible names, and to tell him more cruel lies, but he couldn't, God was preventing him.

'Goodbye,' he said, politely and made for the door.

Outside it his cousins were waiting. They were expecting him to come out cowed and in tears, and were fascinated to see him smiling and cheerful. He took his compass out of his pocket and held it in his hand. They didn't know where they were going but he did.

Four

Two weeks before Christmas his mother became critically ill, so that her sisters came not just to visit her but to see her for the last time. She had begged that they be sent for.

'Fiona, too?' Matthew's father had asked, bitterly.

'Yes, Hugh. Please.'

'But not your father. He wouldn't come anyway.'

Her voice was now reduced to a hoarse, painful whisper.

Matthew had to put his ear close to her mouth.

His father sat by her bedside for hours, looking, by comparison, so strong and healthy, with his blond hair and beard. He couldn't paint because, he said, he hadn't the heart for it. He said it, though, as if he knew he would have plenty of time afterwards to paint.

One day his aunts all arrived. They had met in Aunt Morag's house in Paisley and had come in her car.

They were shocked at how close to death their sister was. They seemed to blame Matthew's father.

'As if your father caused cancer,' said Mrs Macdonald, in the kitchen. 'We ken who caused it, don't we?'

Matthew wondered if she meant God.

*   *   *

The day after his aunts arrived his mother was taken to the hospital in an ambulance. There they could give her drugs to lessen the pain.

Matthew had not gone to school that day. His father had given him permission to stay off.

Aunt Fiona wasn't pleased. 'Better for him to be kept out of the way,' she said.

Mrs Macdonald heard and couldn't keep quiet. 'He's only ten,' she said, 'but he's a human being and he's got feelings. He's no' a cat.'

It seemed to Matthew that Lucy the cat knew something was wrong. She went about with little plaintive mews and wouldn't eat.

His father went in the ambulance with his mother, though she didn't know he was there. He spoke to Mrs Macdonald. 'I want to be with her.'

'She may be unconscious, Mr Sowglass, but she'll ken you're there.'

The aunts were to follow the ambulance in Aunt Morag's car.

'What about me?' asked Matthew.

'You will stay at home,' said Aunt Fiona. 'A hospital is no place for a child.'

'But I want to go. My father said I could.'

His other aunts murmured among themselves that perhaps he should be allowed, but Fiona was adamant. It was for his own good, she said.

He hated her.

In desperation he went to the kitchen. Lucy went with him.

'Whit's the maitter?' asked Mrs Macdonald.

'They're not letting me go.'

'We'll see aboot that.' Mrs Macdonald took him by the hand. Together they went to the big front room where his aunts, hats and gloves on, were ready to leave.

'Whit's this aboot no' letting him go?' she cried.

'What business is it of yours?' said Aunt Fiona, haughtily. 'You're no relative. You're just a servant.'

'I've kent the wean since he was four. I've looked efter him when his poor mither wasn't able. He has a right. He's got the maist right.'

'A hospital is no place for a child.'

But his other aunts weren't so sure.

'In any case there's no room in the car,' said Aunt Fiona.

That was a lie. He could easily squeeze in between his aunts at the back.

'There's plenty of room in mine,' said Mrs Macdonald. 'Hasn't it occurred to you, ladies, that though I'm just a servant I would like to see the poor soul too. I wasn't just her servant, I was her freen'.'

Matthew had noticed how when Mrs Macdonald was excited she spoke Scotch.

So he went with her in her red Mini.

'Will my father come back with us?' he asked, after a long silence.

'I expect so.'

'Maybe he'll want to stay in the hospital with my mother.'

'Maybe he will.'

'Your aunt Fiona' – Mrs Macdonald found words difficult to find – 'didnae mean tae be sae hard-herted. It's juist her way.'

He shook his head. Aunt Fiona *was* hard-hearted. Maybe his grandfather had ordered her to be cruel to Matthew because of his 'diabolical insolence'. Matthew had looked it up in the dictionary.

Looking out of the window he didn't know where they were. The hospital was fifteen miles from Lunderston.

Though it was just half past three it was already dark. He clutched his compass in his pocket.

Suddenly he felt an urgent need to go to the toilet. It was nervousness causing it.

Mrs Macdonald recognised the signs. 'Can you haud oot till we get there?'

'I think so.'

He knew what to do. Think of something else. What, though? Something that had nothing to do with his mother. Then he had it. He'd think of wee Davy Moore, who was in his class at school. He lived in the Glebe, a poor part of the town where all the people lived in council houses. He was a dunce but it didn't bother him. He just grinned. That was why the teacher Miss Johnston often made a fool of him. Matthew hated when she was doing it. He wanted to kill her.

There were few spaces left in the big car park at the hospital. Did it mean that there were many people very ill like his mother?

Mrs Macdonald showed him where the toilet was in the vestibule. He was coming out of it when his aunts arrived.

He saw a girl about his own age, holding her mother's hand. Was it her father who was ill? She looked very unhappy. He would have liked to go up to her and say, well, what could he have said? He could have said 'Good luck.'

As they went up in the big lift, with other people, including the girl and her mother, Matthew considered that some of the people who were very ill would get better but others would die. Who was it decided? Was it God? But how did He decide? Did He decide that good people, like his mother, would live and bad people would die? But didn't good people die too? Perhaps God tossed a coin. But what if there were no coins in heaven. Money wouldn't be needed there.

Going along the corridor that smelled of disinfectant he took off his school-cap and stuffed it into his raincoat pocket.

This was to show respect for the people who were ill. For the same reason he walked very quietly, almost on his tiptoes.

His aunts went in front, he and Mrs Macdonald followed. It was as if they were visiting different patients.

His mother was in a private room in Ward 3B. At the entrance to the ward a nurse in a blue uniform was seated at a table, filling in a form. A plastic card pinned to her breast said her name was M. Watson.

When Aunt Fiona said they had come to see Mrs Sowglass the nurse's smile, directed mainly at Matthew, turned to a frown. 'I'm sorry,' she said, in a professional voice. 'Mrs Sowglass died in the ambulance. Her husband is with her now.'

She spoke as if she wanted to let them know it wasn't her fault, she just worked there.

Again Matthew tried desperately to think about something else. Unfortunately what came into his mind was the beetle he had tried to kill that summer. He drove that out and thought of Pegasus, his big rocking-horse. Often he went galloping on it among the stars.

Luckily he had still his compass to hold on to.

'The dead woman is our sister,' said Aunt Fiona. 'Please take us to see her.'

'Yes, of course.' But the nurse hesitated. She wasn't sure that Matthew's father wanted them to go into his mother's room while he was there.

'Just a minute, please.' The nurse got up and went into the ward.

'He killed her,' said Aunt Fiona.

At first Matthew didn't realise she meant his father.

'Not now, Fiona,' said Aunt Morag. 'Not here.'

'And it's not really true,' whispered Aunt Rachel, the dark-skinned one.

'He caused her to destroy her family.'

'Don't exaggerate, Fiona,' said Aunt Martha, Ailie's mother. 'We're not destroyed.'

'Your father is.'

'Poor Catriona,' whispered Aunt Morag.

The nurse returned. 'Mr Sowglass said I'd to ask the boy if he'd like to see his mother.'

'Of course he does,' said Mrs Macdonald. 'Don't you, Matthew?'

He nodded, but he dreaded it.

'It's all right,' said the nurse. 'Your mother's very peaceful now. You're very like her, aren't you?'

Lots of people had said so: the same jet-black hair, dark-blue eyes, pale skin, and small delicate ears.

What he noticed first in the small room was that his father was wearing a bright-red tie. He kept looking at it, so that he would not have to look at his mother on the bed.

His father said nothing. Neither did Matthew. Matthew was trying not to think about his mother. He thought instead of Davy Moore and discovered, to his surprise, that he loved Davy and wanted to protect him.

'Would you like to say goodbye to your mother?' asked his father.

Matthew nodded, but how did you say goodbye to a dead person who couldn't hear or see?

His father lifted him up. He gazed down at the face which had always been for him the dearest and most familiar in the world. It was peaceful, there was no pain in it now, but it was very still and very far away. He couldn't bear to kiss it but he put out his hand and touched it. He was shocked by its coldness. He hadn't pressed hard, yet there remained a little dent where he had touched.

His father set him down.

His aunts then came in, led by Aunt Fiona.

Mrs Macdonald came staunchly behind them.

It was to her his father spoke. 'I believe Matthew came with you, Mrs Macdonald. Will you give me a lift home?'

'Surely, Mr Sowglass.' Suddenly she was weeping. 'I'm terribly terribly sorry. She was so young.'

Young? thought Matthew. But his mother had been twenty-eight. Mrs Macdonald, though, was sixty-one.

'She didn't have a Christian marriage,' said Aunt Fiona. 'We shall see to it she has a Christian burial.'

His father said nothing but went out with Matthew.

'I'll be wi' you in a minute,' said Mrs Macdonald. 'I'd like to say goodbye.' She was still weeping.

It was strange, thought Matthew, none of his aunts was weeping. They seemed to be afraid to weep.

In the Mini going home Matthew sat beside Mrs Macdonald. His father sat by himself in the back.

Nobody said anything all the way to Lunderston.

Matthew clutched the compass in his pocket. Where was he going now, without his mother?

He kept thinking that they should be doing something to help her. But what could they do? The hospital people would look after her. Then the undertaker. Then, if his father allowed it, the minister. Then God.

Lucy met him in the hall. She didn't want to be lifted and petted, she was too old for that. He bent and patted her. That was enough. She mewed quietly and crept off to one of her favourite corners.

Five

There was a service in St Cuthbert's, which Matthew's father attended, in huffish silence, and a burial in a new grave in Lunderston cemetery, on a cold wet afternoon, which meant that there were few casual onlookers. Most of the McLure clan were there, with Matthew's aunts foremost. There was a row over Matthew but he wasn't told what it was about.

When at last they were all gone and the house was quiet again, his father asked Matthew to come up to the studio, he had something important to say to him.

Matthew consulted Mrs Macdonald in the kitchen. She had been drinking sherry. 'For my nerves,' she muttered.

'Did my father tell you what he wants to say to me?' he asked.

She was uneasy. 'He did and he didnae. I'd raither he telt you himself.'

'Is he not well?'

'He's hert-broken, like you and me.'

Matthew had once heard his father crying at night, but it could have been the gulls that slept on the roof.

'It'll tak him a long time to get ower it,' she said.

Matthew nodded. It would take him a long time too.

'I ken, son, but it's harder for him. When you're aulder you'll ken whit I mean.'

She didn't want to explain or perhaps she couldn't, so he went up the stairs to the studio, very slowly. He didn't weep. He never did. It was because he thought too much.

He knocked.

His father didn't call to him to come in, he came himself and opened the door. Matthew saw that he had been weeping. That was strange, his father in tears and himself dry-eyed. Was it because that he was one of the Chosen, that he didn't, or couldn't, weep?

His father stroked his head. 'Poor Matthew,' he said.

Matthew noticed that the studio had been tidied up. Paintings, finished and unfinished, that had been lying about, were neatly stacked against the walls.

'Sit down, Matthew.'

Matthew sat down on his usual stool. He folded his arms.

His father went and looked out of the big skylight window. It was dark outside. Rain could be heard stotting on the glass.

'What a miserable country this is, isn't it, Matthew?'

Matthew had never known any other, so he couldn't say anything.

'I'm going away, Matthew.'

Matthew considered that curt statement. 'When?'

'The day after tomorrow.'

'Before Christmas?'

'Yes.'

'You'll not be here at Christmas, then?'

'No, I won't. I'm sorry.'

'Where are you going?'

'Somewhere where it's warm and sunny and people know how to be happy.'

Matthew could have said that he knew how to be happy, but he didn't. What he said was: 'Are you going for a while?'

'Aye, for a while, for a very long while.'

'Who'll look after the shop?'

The shop, known as the Gallery, was one of the biggest and most expensive in the main street. It had been established by Matthew's Sowglass grandfather. As well as paintings it sold things like fancy plates and little statues; people bought them for wedding presents . . . His father didn't like the things it sold.

'Miss Carmichael will do that.'

She already was the manageress.

Matthew had kept the most urgent question to the last. 'Are you taking me with you?'

His father kept staring out into the dark.

'I can't do that, Matthew.'

'I'd like to go.'

'You're too young. There's your education to consider.'

'Aren't there schools where you're going?'

'I don't know yet where I'm going. I may be moving about.'

'Will you come back?'

'Yes, of course, I'll come back.'

'Maybe if it's warm and sunny and everybody's happy you'll not want to come back.'

'We'll keep in touch. You can write letters, can't you?'

'Just wee short ones.'

'They'll do. I'll write you long ones.'

'Good.' But Matthew didn't think that promise would be kept.

'Now, Matthew, there's the question of what's to be done with you. Your aunts think you should go and live with one of them. Aunt Martha thinks you would be happy with her and Ailie.'

'I'd like to stay here with Mrs Macdonald.'

'I thought so. So you will then.'

'Will Aunt Fiona try to take me away?'

'I'll make sure she doesn't.'

'Good. Can I go and tell Mrs Macdonald?' He stood up. His father came over to him.

'You know, Matthew, I've never seen you cry. I know you're missing your mother as much as I am, maybe more, but you don't cry.'

Matthew couldn't say: 'The Chosen Ones don't cry.' His father wouldn't understand.

'Don't be afraid to cry.'

Luckily his father gave up then.

Mrs Macdonald felt honoured that she was to be Matthew's guardian. To be honest, she also felt relieved. Some years ago, when she had come to work as a live-in housekeeper, she had had to give up her council flat, so it would have been a great inconvenience for her to find another place to live. Besides, she was proud to live in such a big handsome house on the sea-front. That it was sombrely furnished and old-fashioned suited her. She herself wasn't what you would have called lively and up to date.

All the same, she thought she owed it to Matthew to have a frank talk about his being deserted – that was what it amounted to – by his father, at a time when he most needed his father's company and support.

'I'm very fond of Matthew, Mr Sowglass, and I'll enjoy looking after him, but – excuse me if you think I'm speaking out of turn – doesn't he need you more than he needs me?'

'I know that, Mrs Macdonald, but I can't help it. I have to go. I just can't stand it here any longer. I'd go mad. I'd never be able to paint again.'

Well, imagine that now. Don't let anything stop you painting. He had put it before his wife and now he was putting it before his son. Whether his painting was worth that, Mrs Macdonald couldn't say: she wasn't a good enough judge. She herself didn't much care for his paintings, though she had one, a gift, on her kitchen wall, but then she cared even less for Picasso's and he was said to be the greatest artist of the twentieth century.

'You'll keep in touch,' she said.

'Yes, of course.'

'If you let me know your address I'll see that he writes to you.'

'Thank you. I may be on the move but I'll certainly keep in touch.'

He would have the money for gallivanting. His father had left a considerable fortune and the shop was profitable. Also, to be fair, he made money from his paintings. She had read praise of his work in the *Herald*.

Six

S owglass wasn't the only one who sometimes found life in Lunderston too dull.

Mrs Macdonald had read so many of the romantic novels in the public library that she often found herself taking home ones she'd already read. So she had devised a scheme, whereby she put a secret dot on page 45 of every novel she took out. Even so she was often left in doubt, for most of the stories were very much alike, in that they had handsome well-off heroes and beautiful heroines, who were kept apart by villains or villainesses, or by fatuous misunderstandings. That cold dreary December morning, two days before Christmas, as she watched Hugh Sowglass leave his house en route for Glasgow airport and thereafter to some mysterious far-off destination, she realised that here, before her eyes, was a romantic situation. All the ingredients were there: handsome young painter with blond beard whose wife had just died of cancer and who was in love with a red-haired beauty who kept a flower shop. The latter was Mrs Macdonald's own invention. There *was* a red-haired florist. Her name was Sheila McKenzie but the love affair existed only in Mrs Macdonald's imagination.

There was no place for children in these romances. They brought reality too close.

As she smoked the first of her five cigarettes a day, Mrs

Macdonald let her imagination off the leash. She pictured Sowglass and Sheila, more or less naked, on a tropical beach. A rajah owned the island. His spies brought him reports of the beautiful red-haired Scotswoman. Determined to add her to his harem, he sent turbanned minions to kidnap her. Exchanging his paint brush for a scimitar her lover set out through the jungle to rescue her.

At that point Isabel Macdonald, the romanticist, was shoved out of the way by Bella Macdonald, the realist. What bloody nonsense, said Bella. What was the reality? Sowglass was a weak selfish man running away from his responsibilities. Sheila McKenzie was engaged to marry a member of the Rotary Club of Lunderston, and she herself was a past president of the Lunderston Women's Business Club.

Outside it was cold and wet. She almost sympathised with Sowglass.

'I'd better run you along to the school,' she said.

'Do I have to go?' asked Matthew.

She had been instructed that he must attend school regularly, but, for God's sake, his mother had been buried three days ago and his father that very morning had abandoned him, how could he be expected to concentrate on sums and spelling?

'No, you don't,' she said. 'We'll do some Christmas shopping.'

'Can we buy a Christmas tree?'

'Why not?'

A Christmas tree stood for faith in ordinary things and ordinary people. Everybody would be buying them. That was the kind of faith she must encourage in him. He mustn't be let think that his mother's death had set him apart.

They left the Mini in the car park on the sea-front and walked along the main street, in watery sunshine, the rain having gone off for the time being. The main street was said by

Lunderstonians to be one of the most splendid in the country: so much so that the town had once sought to be twinned with the Californian resort of Palm Springs, that haunt of millionaires, which also had bye-laws obliging shopkeepers and others to keep their premises looking smart and prosperous.

Having lived in the town for over thirty years Mrs Macdonald was bound to meet acquaintances. They were interested in her small companion but were too well mannered to embarrass him with condolences. One or two, noted for their uncontrollable nosiness, would have pestered him with solicitous questions if she hadn't cut them off. Always at the back of her mind was the dread that he might break down. It could be a collapse that might last all his life.

They passed the Gallery. Miss Carmichael, dressed in black, saw them through the window. She gave them a wave.

They came to the florist's. There was Sheila, clad in tartan skirt and Fair-Isle jumper, dealing with a customer. Her nose, and her hands, were too big for a romantic heroine's.

There were Christmas trees on display. Matthew led the way in.

Miss McKenzie came forward to greet them.

Her blue eyes were too sensible. There was no mystery in them. She was what Sowglass had fled from. If Mrs Macdonald had been a painter she wouldn't have wanted to paint her.

Miss McKenzie could have left it to her assistants, but she herself explained to Matthew about Christmas trees. This was a Douglas fir, that a Scots pine, and this a Norway spruce. She recommended the last. Its needles were easy to handle.

Mrs Macdonald had a word in private with her while Matthew was looking at some hideous garden gnomes. Probably Miss McKenzie thought they were hideous but she had customers who liked them and bought them, therefore she stocked them.

'Do you ken who he is?' whispered Mrs Macdonald.

'Mr Sowglass's son?' Mrs Sowglass's, too.

'Poor child. It's as well he's young. I mean, at his age, he can't really be aware of what's happened to him.'

'He's got a lot to be aware of. His faither left this morning.'

'You mean, went away?'

'Yes.'

'Where to?'

'He didn't say. He just said he had to get away from Lunderston.'

'I think he'll find there are worse places than Lunderston.'

There was a touch of Aunt Fiona about her. That rajah would have rued kidnapping her. She'd have reorganised his harem for him.

The Christmas tree and some holly with berries on it were to be sent to the house. They would be duly delivered.

In the car going home he said: 'Do you know what I would like?'

She smiled. He was the least greedy wean she had ever known. 'No. What would you like?'

'I'd like someone to come to the house and play with me.'

'One of your friends?'

'Well, a sort of friend.'

'What's his name?'

'Davy Moore.'

'I don't think I've heard you talking about him.'

'He's in my class at school.'

'What does his father do?'

That typical Scots question.

'I don't think he does anything.'

'I see. Where does he live, this Davy Moore?'

'In the Glebe.'

'The Glebe?'

It was the one disreputable part of the town. 'But it's only scruff that live there.' Immediately she regretted saying that.

Who was she, who used to live in a council flat herself, though in a respectable area, to call people scruff? Still, the Glebe did have a reputation for drunken affrays, vandalism, mangy dogs, and undisciplined children.

'Isn't there somebody else you could invite?'

'No. I want Davy.'

'Why do you want him?'

He couldn't tell her it was because he loved Davy Moore and wanted to protect him. It would have sounded stupid.

'What's he like, this Davy Moore? Is he clever?'

'No, he's not clever.'

'Are you telling me he's a dunce?'

'Yes. But he doesn't mind. He's always laughing.'

'Sounds very like a dunce, I must say.'

It was necessary to tell the truth. 'He used to steal things in Woolworth's.'

'Good heavens!'

'I don't think he does it any more.'

'I should hope not. I don't think your father would want you to have a boy like that for a friend.'

He gave that some thought. 'I don't think he'd mind.'

No, he wouldn't, and to be fair not because he couldn't be bothered minding. One thing that Sowglass was not was a snob. Didn't he have prostitutes off the street to paint them?

'Well, *I* mind.' But she couldn't say it with conviction. If Matthew had Christian impulses it wasn't for her or for anyone to crush them. 'But I'll think about it.'

The car then stopped at the house.

'Some day during the holidays would do,' he said.

'We'll see.'

'I could write to him. He's not very good at reading but I wouldn't use big words.'

'That's right, no big words.'

She found it funny, he didn't.

She hoped, cravenly, that in a day or two he would have dropped the idea.

In the meantime she tried to find out something about the Moores.

She telephoned her friend, Maggie Oliphant, who worked in the Oxfam shop and knew everything that went on in Lunderston.

At first, though, Maggie herself was inquisitive.

'Is it true, Bella, that Sowglass has gone away?'

'Mr Sowglass has gone away for a while to try and get over his wife's daith.'

'And left the boy behind?'

'Behind in my care. I'm telephoning, Maggie, to ask if you can tell me anything about a family called Moore that lives in the Glebe.'

'You'd have thought he'd have taken the boy with him.'

'What sort of people are these Moores?'

Maggie laughed. 'All right. I'll mind my own business. What do you want to know about the Moores for? I hope you've not fallen foul of big Jessie.'

'I've never met the woman. It seems she has a son called Davy. Matthew wants to invite him to the house to play. I'm no' sure whether I should allow it or no'.'

'He's a wee rascal, Davy Moore.'

'In what way a rascal? Is he a thief? I heard he's a shoplifter.'

'Who told you that?'

'Never mind who. Is it true?'

'If it is it would be more mischief than dishonesty. Jessie would murder him if she found him stealing. When she comes into the shop she'll demand a reduction in price but she pays for everything she gets. Unlike some so called ladies in this town, I can tell you. Big Jessie's not braw but she's honest.'

'Is there a Mr Moore?'

'There is, called Charlie I believe. From what I've heard he's a cheery good-natured sort. He's got a bad leg: an accident when he was a child. They're a funny pair but I believe they get on well. I don't think it would do your boy any harm having Davy to play with. It might do him good. I've heard Matthew's a sad wee soul.'

'His mother has just died, Maggie.'

'That's so.'

'Well, thanks for the information, Maggie. I'll think it over.'

She thought it over, sipping sherry and smoking her second-last cigarette of the day. She gave him her decision at teatime.

'You can have this Davy Moore to play with you.'

'Oh good.'

'They haven't got a phone, so you'll have to write.'

'What day shall I say? Would the day after Christmas do?'

'Why not?'

So, when the table was cleared, he sat at it writing the letter. Often he paused to think, tapping his nose with his pen. Mrs Macdonald took care not to go so close as to make him suspect she was trying to spy. If he showed it to her she would be pleased. If he didn't she would respect his privacy.

He was about to address the envelope when he realised he didn't know Davy's exact address.

'Would Davy Moore, the Glebe, do?' he asked.

It would depend on whether the postman knew the Glebe as well as the police did.

'We could go to the library and look at the Voters' Roll,' she said.

'That would take time.'

'It would.'

'I'll just put the Glebe.'

'That'll probably get him all right.'

'This is what I've written. "Dear Davy, I would like very much if you could come and play with me on December 26th, that's the day after Christmas. Please let me know if you can come. Yours truly, Matthew Sowglass." Will that do?'

'It'll do fine. How is he to let you know? Can he write?'

'He's not a very good speller. Maybe his big brother Joe will help him.'

'Has he got a big brother Joe?'

'Yes. When Davy got the belt from Mr Buchanan, the headmaster, he was going to get his big brother Joe to come to the school and kick Mr Buchanan's erse.'

'I hope Joe did.'

'No, he didn't.'

He insisted on going out to post the letter. There was a pillar-box not far from the house. Luckily, Lunderston was still a place where it was safe for children and women to walk after dark.

Lucy often went walking with him. This evening she ran after him to the door, looked out, felt the cold, sniffed the damp, and hurried back in. Cats, thought Mrs Macdonald, were survivors because they considered only their own needs.

He was soon back. She helped him off with his raincoat.

'Did you get it posted all right?'

'Yes, thank you.'

Later, just before his bedtime, they were in the kitchen, Mrs Macdonald reading a romance and Matthew concentrating on a jigsaw, when he suddenly asked: 'When you were a little girl, Mrs Macdonald, were you happy?'

My God, what a question, she thought, but since it had been asked seriously she felt obliged to give it an adequate answer.

'I think so, but when we look back it's the happy times we seem to remember, no' the miserable ones.'

'Were you sometimes miserable?'

Jolted back to childhood, she could have wept, not for

herself as she was now, a failed old woman of sixty-one, but for the eager little girl she had been all those years ago.

'There was one time. But, if you'll excuse me, I'd raither no' talk aboot it.'

'Is it a secret?'

'Aye, it's a secret.'

'I wouldn't tell anybody.'

She smiled. 'We were living in Glasgow, in Dalgleish Street. A telegram came. It was to tell us, my mither and me, that my faither had been killed in the War. I was aboot your age then. In Mesopotamia.'

'I didn't know your father was killed in the War, Mrs Macdonald.'

'No' the last war. The one before it. The war that was to end all wars.'

Since then there had been many, with many more deaths. There was one being fought today.

'I'm sorry,' he said.

'It was a long time ago.'

'I've got a secret too.'

'I promise I'll no' tell onyone.'

'Did you know, Mrs Macdonald, that there are special people chosen by God?'

She had to smile, he had said it so solemnly. But it was nothing to smile at. For God's sake, son, she thought, don't take after your grandfather, don't let religion ruin your life as it did his, aye, and your poor mother's.

She tried to make a joke of it. 'Do you mean, rich people, like the Duke of Buccleuch?'

'I don't think they have to be rich. They were chosen before they were born, before the world began.'

'Was it your grandfather told you this?'

'Yes. People who are chosen get pardoned. Even if they killed someone they would be pardoned.'

'By God, maybe, but people who weren't chosen would hang them.'

'No, they couldn't. God wouldn't let them.'

Mrs Macdonald wasn't altogether ignorant. She had lived in Scotland all her life. She had heard about the Calvinist doctrine of predestination. John Knox had believed in it, but surely nobody did today, except a few crazy bigots, like that old man in the Outer Hebrides.

It wasn't a joke, though. There could be danger in it.

'I think I'm one of the Chosen. When I killed a beetle last summer nothing happened.'

What in God's name had he expected to happen?

'It's your conscience that tells you if what you've done is right or wrong, isn't it?'

'It's supposed to.'

'People who are chosen don't need a conscience. They're always right, you see.'

No, she didn't see. It was terrible nonsense.

Yet didn't nations do wicked things and claim that they had a right to do them, a right given them by God? Wasn't this war in Vietnam an example? Just a few evenings ago she had seen on television a child younger than Matthew running along a road, its body on fire, caused by chemicals dropped by American planes. Those pilots would say they had God's permission and therefore God's pardon. They would expect praise, not blame.

Matthew was smiling. God forgive her, it seemed a sinister smile.

If it had been his teeth giving him trouble she could have taken him to a dentist, but who could she take him to if it was his mind or his soul that needed treatment? There were five ministers in the town, six if you counted the Pentecostal Church, but how could she explain to them about this daft, this diabolical, belief that seemed to have taken root in

Matthew's mind? Old Mr Henderson of St Cuthbert's, where she and Matthew worshipped, would say, so sensibly but so inadequately, not to worry, it was just a childish fancy caused by misunderstanding, and he would grow out of it.

She told herself not to be silly, but from now on she was going to find it difficult not to look on him more anxiously.

On Christmas Day, after lunch, the telephone rang. Wearing a paper party hat Matthew rushed into the hall to answer it. He shouted that it might be his father.

It wasn't his father's voice but at first he wasn't sure whether it was a man's or a woman's, it was so rough and deep.

'Wha's this?' it asked.

'It's me, Matthew Sowglass. If it's my father you want he's gone abroad.'

'Was it you sent that letter to my Davy?'

'Are you Mrs Moore? Yes, it was me. Can Davy come?'

She laughed. 'Why d'you want him? You and he are no special freen's, are you?'

He said nothing but he nodded. They were special friends.

'Look, son, is there somebody I can talk to? Is there somebody looking efter you?'

'Mrs Macdonald is looking after me.'

'Richt. Tell her I'd like to talk to her. And for God's sake, son, get a move on. I'm in a phonebox and it's freezing cauld.'

He ran to the kitchen. 'It's Mrs Moore.'

'Mrs Moore?'

'Yes. Davy's mother. She wants to talk to you. She says hurry because she's in a phonebox and it's freezing cold.'

'Is that so?'

Wiping her hands with her apron Mrs Macdonald went off to put this impatient hussy in her place. She spoke into the telephone with exaggerated properness. 'Isabel Macdonald speaking.'

'Jessie Moore here, Davy's mither. It's aboot that letter. Are we to tak it seriously? You ken whit weans are like.'

'Yes, you are to take it seriously. Matthew is very keen to have your boy to play with him.'

'Is he lonely? Is he missing his mither? Is that it? I was very sorry to hear aboot that. My ain mither died some months back. Davy was very fond of his granny.'

Mrs Macdonald relaxed. Mrs Moore might be scruff but she evidently had human feelings. 'Yes, Matthew is very upset, but he knows what he's doing. Does your boy want to come?'

'Davy's game for onything. Will you be there?'

'Yes, I'll be here.'

'Good. Then he'll come. Thanks for inviting him.'

'Shall we pick him up at two o'clock tomorrow afternoon?'

'He'll be ready. You ken whaur we live?'

'The Glebe, isn't it?'

'That's right. Whaur the closes are knee deep in dogs' shite.' Mrs Moore laughed: she was being ironic. If that was what the toffs on the sea-front thought, let them. 'Laverock Terrace, no. 3. Ken whit Laverock means? It means skylark. Whit a laugh.' And she laughed.

Mrs Moore would have liked to go in style in Mr Sowglass's big green Audi, but she wasn't sure she could drive it, So they went in her old Mini, which, battered and rusted, wouldn't be a temptation to vandals.

Once in the Glebe they drove slowly along Laverock Terrace, seeing a few sparrows but no skylarks. At close no. 3 Davy was waiting, with his mother. He was wearing a Glasgow Rangers' scarf, tammy to match, blue jeans, big boots, and a red and blue jerkin. Every garment looked freshly washed, as did his face, which, though puckish, was cheerful. He carried a brown paper parcel, no doubt a present for Matthew. No Scot ever went visiting without a present.

Mrs Macdonald felt relieved. He might be an ex-shoplifter,

but he was normal. In Woolworth's it would be the manager he would be on the look-out for, not God.

His mother was a big buxom woman with a heavy face. She was wearing a bright-red jumper. She looked and smelled passably clean. A glance into the close showed no depth of dogs' mess.

Davy was given stern but affectionate last instructions.

'Mind whit I said aboot lifting things that don't belong to you.'

He nodded, unabashed. To Matthew he said: 'Can I get a shot on your hoarse?'

'Hoarse?' cried his mother. 'My God, I didnae ken you had a hoarse.'

'It's a wooden one,' said Mrs Macdonald.

Some of Davy's friends had gathered round, inquisitively. A little girl of about five, neatly dressed, with blue empty eyes, said: 'Can I go in the caur wi' you, Davy?'

Mrs Moore picked her up and hugged her. 'No' this time, Veronica, hen.'

Mrs Macdonald wondered what kind of life lay ahead of a child with a name like that and those blank eyes.

'She's no' wice,' said Davy, tapping his brow, as he got into the car.

'Is she your sister?' asked Mrs Macdonald.

'Naw, she's nae relative, we're a' wice.'

They drove off.

'See that wee dug peeing against the lamp-post,' cried Davy. 'Its name's Prince. It's no' weel. Sometimes it howls a' night.'

There was no pity or condemnation in his voice, only interest. Davy was interested in everything.

What at first annoyed Mrs Macdonald a little but soon amused and finally pleased her was how their guest, though appreciative of the superiority of the spacious villa to his own cramped council flat, was not a bit subdued or overwhelmed or envious. When admiring the stag's head in the hall he remarked that in the Glasgow Art Galleries he had once seen a lifesize model of a dinosaur. Introduced to Lucy, who shrank back when he attempted to stroke her, he confessed that he sometimes threw stones at cats, so he couldn't blame her for not trusting him, could he?

Mrs Macdonald overheard a conversation between him and Matthew, about Matthew's mother. Davy had been admiring her photograph on the piano in the big front room.

'Was that your mither?' he asked.

'Yes.'

'You look like her. Did you ken that?'

Matthew nodded.

'Why is she no' smiling? People are supposed to smile when they get their photies taken. The man likes them to smile. But maybe she wasn't feeling weel.'

'I don't know.'

'Did you see her deid?'

'Yes.'

'In her coaffin?'

'No. In the hospital.'

'My granny dee'd in the hospital. She had a heart attack. Did your mither have a heart attack?'

'No. She had cancer.'

'I think that's worse. Dae you ken whit I think. I think deid folk are ca'd away. They hear a voice naebody else does. It tells them they've to go.'

'Go where?'

'Naebody kens that.'

'What voice do they hear?'

'Naebody kens that either. You'd hae to be deid to ken that. I went to the hospital to see my granny. She didnae speak to

me. She didnae speak to onybody. But I could tell she was
listening, tae the voice.'

Well, thought Mrs Macdonald, wasn't that what the ministers said; only they said it more importantly and less convin-
cingly.

'This should be a good hoose for ghosts,' said Davy. 'Mine
isnae. It's too wee. Ghosts like hooses wi' lots o' rooms. Have
you see your mither's ghost?'

'No.'

'If you dae don't ask it onything. Ghosts don't like you to
ask them things. They're no' allowed to tell you. They've got
to keep their secrets.'

What were those secrets? She had asked Angus, her husband, and wee Anabel, her daughter, both long since dead,
but neither had answered.

She felt tears in her eyes. She could easily love this little
boy who spoke so cheerfully and knowledgeably about the
dead.

Later, when they were eating, Davy eating twice as much as
Matthew, he told them about another of his beliefs Had they
seen pictures on television of starving black kids, with bellies
like drums and legs and arms like spurtles? If he could he
would have shared his food with them, but he couldn't, so he
ate their share too, otherwise it would go to waste. His granny
had often told him it was a sin to waste food.

Mrs Macdonald asked him about school. How did he like it?

It was all right, he said, except that his teacher Miss
Johnston was a cunt. Perhaps, his tone conceded, that was
a swear word that Mrs Macdonald might not like, but he
couldn't help it. What other word was there to describe Miss
Johnston? She knew he was a dunce, he knew it himself,
everybody in the class knew it, so why did she go on about it all
the time? He could do things she couldn't, like playing a
mouth organ, and he knew things she didn't, like the number

of times the Rangers had won the league. But he didn't go about saying she was stupid and ignorant, did he?

He asked for a shot on the hobby-horse. He didn't, as Matthew had feared, stay on it for a long time. He didn't want to tire it out, he said. He said it so seriously that Matthew wasn't sure whether or not he was joking.

He asked if she could see Matthew's father's paintings. Mrs Macdonald hesitated at first but she could see no harm in it, so she accompanied him and Matthew up to the studio.

He just looked, careful not to touch anything. He offered no comments on any of the paintings, not even those of naked women. He himself liked painting, he said, and he was quite good at it. That was something Miss Johnston never gave him credit for. She said that when he drew and painted a teapot he made the handle too big and the spout too thin, but since it was his painting he could make them any size he liked, couldn't he? Some of the scuddy women in Mr Sowglass's paintings were fat and their skin was more blue than white, but if Mr Sowglass wanted them fat and blue then he had a right, for it was his painting. The trouble with Miss Johnston was that she had 'nae imagination'.

His father, he said, was a champion domino player. He played for a pub team. His pub was the Auld Hoose. It was top of the league last season.

His mother was a great dancer, he said. She said herself she was too heavy nowadays, but he had seen her fox-trotting in the Queen's Hall and she had been one of the best fox-trotters there.

His big brother Joe was a message boy for Murray the butcher. He went round with the delivery van. When he was promoted he would get cutting up carcases. That's what you called 'deid coos'.

What was Davy himself going to be? Maybe a painter. Not the kind like Matthew's father who painted pictures, but the kind that decorated houses. He had helped his mother to choose the wallpaper for their living-room.

'Thanks a million,' he said, as he got out of the car at his close, carrying the bundle of comics Matthew had given him.

He had given Matthew a book about Glasgow Rangers.

He gave them a wave before he disappeared into the close.

'Well,' said Mrs Macdonald, as she drove off, 'he's a terrible wee blether but there's no harm in him.'

'He took my compass.'

She almost stopped the car. 'How could he do that? You've always got it in your pocket.'

'I showed it to him. He asked if he could hold it for a while. He didn't give it back.'

'Why didn't you ask him for it?'

'I couldn't.'

'Why couldn't you?'

'I couldn't.'

'I thought your compass meant a lot to you.'

'That's why, you see.'

She didn't see. 'His mother will make him give it back.'

'He won't let her see it. He won't let anyone see it. He thinks it's magic.'

She had to smile. So did he think it was magic.

Part Two

One

Matthew waited, anxiously, every day, for a letter or postcard from his father. There weren't many, and they never told him much. One thing they never said was when his father was coming home again. The first one came from San Francisco, and then, growing fewer all the time, from places in Mexico: Mexico City, Cuernavaca, Taxco, Guanajuato, and finally Villahermosa, where his father seemed to have settled down. Eagerly Matthew sought out those towns in the big atlas, and read about Mexico in the *Children's Encyclopedia*. Villahermosa interested him most. On the postcards it looked beautiful, with red-tiled white houses and green jungle, but it also looked very remote.

'What's he doing in a place like that?' asked Mrs Macdonald. 'He'll ken nobody there.'

'Maybe he'll get to know people.'

'Maybe. He didn't get to know many here. Why doesn't he write you a long letter giving you all his news?'

'I don't think he likes writing letters.'

'Why doesn't he give you an address so that you can write to him?'

'Maybe he hasn't found a house yet.'

Mrs Macdonald had gathered from a woman she knew who

worked in the office of Mr Baird the lawyer, that Sowglass had money sent to him every month.

To be fair, though, there were times, with rain pelting down, when she envied Sowglass. In a beautiful warm sunny place he was doing what he wanted most of all to do. She might have given him her blessing if it hadn't been for his neglect of Matthew.

There were times when she wondered if he would ever come back. Perhaps, when Matthew was older, he would have to go in search of his father. Mrs Macdonald would have liked to go with him, but she'd likely be too old by then.

Davy Moore was not invited to the house again. He wouldn't be while he held on to the compass.

It began to worry Matthew that he never gave God a chance to show that he was one of the Chosen. He never did anything really wicked. Once he stole a small elephant from the Gallery, but it wasn't really stealing for in a way it belonged to him. Besides, he didn't want the girl who assisted Miss Carmichael to get the blame, so he slily returned it.

Four swans appeared in the sea in front of his house. He thought of throwing stones at them, but couldn't: he liked and admired them too much. Indeed, he got into a quarrel with two other boys when he tried to prevent them from throwing stones. They were bigger than him, so he couldn't stop them, but the swans were too far away to be hit.

He considered dropping a lighted match into a pillar-box, as he had seen other boys doing; but he knew how important letters were to people and he couldn't bring himself to do it.

If he didn't make use of his privilege, would it be taken from him? Perhaps he wasn't really one of the Chosen. Another test was needed.

One sunny May morning, when all the pupils were in the playground, during the interval, he slipped into the school and into his classroom, which was Miss Johnston's classroom, for she was still his teacher, and wrote on the blackboard, in block letters: MISS JOHNSTON IS A CUNT, and then slipped out again without being seen.

It wasn't that she had been particularly harsh that morning. In fact, recently she had looked too tired to be stern, and she had more or less given up being nasty to Davy Moore.

Some other boy, or girl, for girls too used that word nowadays, might get the blame. In that case Matthew would own up. It would be interesting to see how God got him out of it.

The girls came into the classroom first. Immediately they noticed the writing on the blackboard. They were staring at it with horror-stricken gasps or nervous giggles when the boys arrived.

Most of the boys laughed, in delight. Confident in their own innocence, they were going to enjoy Miss Johnston's anger and disgust and her efforts to find out who had done it. They shouted in protest when Elizabeth McFadyen, daughter of the Baptist Church minister, hurried out to the blackboard, apparently with the intention of wiping out that delectable obscenity. She was ordered to leave it alone. Face white as chalk, she crept back to her seat and covered her eyes with her hands.

There was complete silence when Miss Johnston came in, not, these days, with the old brisk menace. She saw them all looking at the blackboard and looked at it herself. She did not scream or rush for the duster. She seemed too tired, too dispirited, too confused.

Then, as they all watched in fascination, one of them laughed. It was Davy Moore. It wasn't spiteful or sarcastic laughter. It was as if he had been told a good joke, the point of which he had just seen. There was even an element of sympathy in his laughter, for though it was undeniable that Miss Johnston was a cunt, still she was old, and her hair was grey, like his granny's who had died not long ago.

Most of his classmates, already suspecting him, thought that his laughter proved it. This was Davy the dunce getting his own back for all the insults.

One or two of the more intelligent wondered how the dunce could have spelled all the words correctly.

They waited for Miss Johnston to grab him and rush him along the corridor to the headmaster.

Instead she said, not very angrily: 'You find this funny, David Moore?'

He thought she was just asking his opinion. He grinned, matily. 'A wee bit,' he said.

He looked about him to see if he could pick out the jolly prankster who was responsible.

'Is it your idea of a joke?' she asked, with a strange weariness.

Since it was, he again grinned and nodded.

Then to his astonishment and everybody's consternation she burst into tears.

'If you think it was me, Miss Johnston,' he said, 'you're wrang. Honest to God.'

She tried to control herself. She dabbed her eyes with her handkerchief.

'I hope you're telling the truth, David,' she said.

'He isn't. He's lying. I saw him do it.'

They looked in astonishment and indignation at the girl who had spoken. She was on her feet. Sheila Burnside was a newcomer to the school and to the town. She had come from Glasgow just three weeks ago. Her father was the new Sheriff Clerk. She was tall for her age and held herself very straight. Her long yellow hair was tied with a red ribbon. She was wearing red jeans. She had made no friends.

They thought that she was clyping and despised her for it. Matthew knew she was also lying. Her eyes looked pitiless. They reminded him of his cat Lucy's. Why was she showing

48

this hatred of poor Davy, who had never even spoken to her? But then, judging by her contemptuous sneer, she hated them all; except, he suddenly realised, himself. When their eyes met her smile changed; it became friendly. It was as if she knew he was the guilty one but was determined to protect him. Was she the agent God had decided to use?

'I left my handkerchief in my bag,' she said. 'I came in to get it. I saw him writing that on the blackboard.'

It was more than Davy could bear. 'You're a fucking liar,' he cried. 'How could you see me when it wisnae me?'

Surely, they all thought, that obscenity proved him guilty. Matthew stood up. 'It wasn't Davy,' he said. 'It was me.'

Nobody believed him. Who could ever mistake Matthew Sowglass for wee Davy Moore? Matthew's clothes were expensive, Davy's cheap. Matthew had black hair, Davy's was dirty-fair. In any case Matthew was a goody-goody; didn't he go to church every Sunday? He never swore, was always clean, had good manners, and was far too clever to write that stupidity on the blackboard.

'Please sit down, Matthew,' said Miss Johnston. 'It's kind of you to try and protect this foolish boy, but you should not lie about it.'

'I don't need onybody to protect me,' cried Davy. 'I didnae dae it.'

Matthew was watching a presence in the room that no one else saw or felt. God's. He was waiting to see how God would settle the matter, in such a way that Matthew came to no harm and Davy wasn't punished for something he hadn't done.

It was settled in a way that only God could have achieved.

Miss Johnston went to her desk at the front and asked a boy there to come out and clean the blackboard.

They all watched in awe as he did it. They thought she would have left it as evidence to show the headmaster.

She picked up an arithmetic book. 'Page 39,' she said. 'Exercise 20. Do the odd numbers only.'

'But, Miss Johnston,' cried two or three, 'we did those this morning.'

'Did you? I'm sorry. How silly of me.'

They were aghast at her accusing herself of silliness.

She got to her feet, with difficulty. 'Excuse me, but I'm afraid I don't feel well.'

Trying to walk with dignity she left the room.

Matthew remembered what Mrs Macdonald had said when he had told her how unfair and unkind the teacher was to Davy Moore.

'Maybe the poor woman's not well.'

It looked as if Mrs Macdonald had been right.

Half an hour later the headmaster came to take the class. Miss Johnston, he said, had had to go home, she wasn't feeling well. He said nothing about the writing on the blackboard, so perhaps she hadn't mentioned it to him.

Two

He had no idea where in Lunderston she lived but knew that it wasn't in his own area on the sea-front, so he was surprised when, as he was walking home after four o'clock in the sunshine, Sheila Burnside stole up and walked beside him. She didn't ask if he minded. She didn't care whether he minded or not. If he didn't get rid of her now he never would.

She had lied when she had said she'd seen Davy writing on the blackboard. She had seen no one. She had just told a brazen and malicious lie. It had given her pleasure. She liked to get harmless people like Davy into trouble. If she'd been one of the Chosen she'd have caused God great difficulty in pardoning and protecting her. But then, would anyone like her ever be chosen? Only by the Devil.

It was nonsense to think of the Devil on such a bright afternoon, with clear blue skies, but when he glanced aside and saw her smiling evilly at him it didn't seem nonsense at all. He should have told her he didn't want her to walk with him, he didn't want her to be his friend. But he couldn't. The truth was he was afraid of her, even though he was under God's protection. Hadn't his grandfather told him the Devil was more powerful than God? That was why there was so much more evil in the world than good.

'Your name's Sowglass, isn't it?' she said.

He said nothing. He didn't even nod.

'That's a funny name, Sowglass. Your family owns that big shop in the main street.'

Again he was silent. He hoped she would take the hint and go.

'Your father's an artist, isn't he?'

At this mention of his father he felt sad and even more afraid.

'He's abroad, isn't he?'

'Yes.'

'Your mother's dead, isn't she?'

'Yes.'

'So's mine. My father killed her.'

As Matthew, shocked, wondered what to make of that monstrous accusation, she added, in the same matter-of-fact tone: 'That's why I'm going to kill him.'

She must be mad, he thought.

She took a packet of cigarettes out of her shoulder bag. She offered him one.

It amazed him that she could be in some ways so childish.

'You don't believe me, do you?'

'No, I don't. Why do you say such silly things?'

She laughed. 'I'm not going to shoot him. I haven't got a gun. I'm not going to cut his throat while he's asleep. I'm going to push him overboard. He's got a sailing boat, you see. Sometimes I act as his crew. It will be easy, especially if there's a storm.'

They arrived at his house. She knew it was his. He wondered how she knew.

There was a seat on the esplanade.

'Let's sit down,' she said.

Two old ladies were passing.

She dropped the cigarette and put her foot on it.

They gave her, this lovely girl with the long fair hair, admiring glances.

She smiled back, respectfully.

They were happy. With children like her, Lunderston was a lucky and happy place.

'I hate old people,' she said. 'They're useless. They're ugly. They should all be dead.'

His swans were there, proud and beautiful. He felt reassured.

'If I'd a gun I'd shoot them,' she said. 'Wouldn't it be fun to see their feathers red with blood?'

'No, it wouldn't. They're doing you no harm.'

'That's what you think.'

He couldn't help being fascinated as to why she thought the swans, so innocent, so beautiful, and so mindful of their own peaceful business, were doing her harm.

Suddenly he knew. Everything that was good, everything that was in its own proper place, was hateful to her, as it was to the Devil.

What did he have that could protect him from her? His compass. But it was protecting Davy Moore.

'That old bitch, Miss Johnston,' she said. 'I hope she dies, in great pain.'

Yet Miss Johnston had never been unpleasant to her. She had praised her for her cleverness.

What, he wondered, had caused her to be like this, preferring evil to good? Had it been her mother's death? How had her mother died? He refused to believe she had been murdered. What age had Sheila been then?

When his own mother had died he had been in danger of hating everybody too, but only for a little while.

Suppose, though, he hadn't been lucky in having his father and Mrs Macdonald and, yes, his compass, to help him back to normal. Would he have been like Sheila, wanting his own back on everybody and everything? Perhaps, making everything too complicated, she needed to be pitied.

She stood up.

'Do you know what I would like?' she said. 'I'd like to see inside your house.'

There it was, his home, where he felt safe. Its name was in gold letters on the glass above the front door. Dunvegan. In the roof was the large skylight of his father's studio.

As he thought of his father tears came into his eyes. He turned his head away so that she wouldn't see them.

'Who looks after you?' she asked.

'Mrs Macdonald.'

'Who's she? A relative?'

'No.'

'Just a servant?'

He never thought of Mrs Macdonald as a servant. She was his friend.

Before he could stop her, or try to, she was crossing the road and going through the gate.

'Maybe it's not convenient,' he said, behind her.

He was appalled at the thought of her taking all the magic, all the goodness, and all the reassurance, out of the things he loved, such as the stag's head, his mother's photograph, and Pegasus, his rocking-horse.

Mrs Macdonald had the front door open and greeted them eagerly. She was pleased to see that he had brought a friend: a friend, too, who didn't look as if she came from the Glebe.

'Hello. I'm Sheila Burnside.'

Seeing her through Mrs Macdonald's eyes he realised how attractive Sheila could look and sound, with her long fair hair, blue eyes, and her lack of shyness, which wasn't the same as impertinence.

Mrs Macdonald was charmed. She saw in this friendly, outgoing, tall girl what her Anabel might have been at the same age, though to be honest both she and Angus her husband had come from small stock, hardly likely to produce a beauty like this.

She showed Sheila into the big front room which was reserved for special visitors. 'I'll put the kettle on and we'll have tea.'

'Thank you, Mrs Macdonald.'

'Show your friend where the bathroom is,' said Mrs Macdonald as she went out.

Sheila laughed. 'Well, where is it?'

'Upstairs.'

But apparently she didn't need.

He did, though. It showed how anxious he was.

She had pushed herself into his life and now she had pushed herself into his home. He wanted to tell her to leave, but he couldn't, he had to be polite and hospitable. Was that why evil so often won, because goodness had to be goodness?

'Is that your mother?' she asked, going over to stare at the photograph on the piano. 'You're very like her.'

She sat down at the piano and began to play.

It astonished Matthew by being quiet, sad music. It reminded him of his mother.

Mrs Macdonald, coming in with a laden tray, was enchanted. She stood listening.

'That was beautiful,' she said. 'Wasn't it, Matthew? What's it called, Sheila?'

'It hasn't got a name. I made it up.'

Mrs Macdonald could scarcely believe it, but Matthew knew that Sheila, who loved lies, was this time speaking the truth. It must have been the Devil who had given her this gift of composing beautiful music. What other gifts had he given her?

'You've got a wonderful talent,' said Mrs Macdonald. 'Hasn't she, Matthew? You could make music your career.'

Sheila got up. 'May I help?' She poured the tea. 'I like music. I've liked it since my mother died.'

'Oh. When was that?'

'Three years ago.'

'I'm very sorry. Have you any sisters or brothers?'

'No.'

'So it's just you and your father?'

'Yes.'

'What does your father do?'

'He's the Sheriff Clerk.'

'I see.'

'These are delicious pancakes, Mrs Macdonald. Did you make them yourself?

'Yes. Matthew's fond of my pancakes. Are you in the same class in school?'

'Yes. Our teacher, Miss Johnston, had to be taken home this morning. She looked very ill. Didn't she, Matthew?'

Her voice was full of sympathy. He remembered her saying she hoped Miss Johnston died in great pain.

'I'd like to go and visit her,' she said. 'Would you come with me, Matthew?'

'I'm sure he would,' said Mrs Macdonald, 'but you'd better wait until we hear how the poor woman is.'

'We could take her flowers.'

'That would be nice.'

Sheila looked about her. 'I don't see a photograph of your father, Matthew.'

'Mr Sowglass didn't like to have his photograph taken,' said Mrs Macdonald, 'but there's a painting of him, done by himself, in Matthew's room.'

'I'd like to see it. Is it like him?'

'Aye, in some ways it's like him. Matthew will take you up to see it.'

But Matthew didn't want to. He felt he had to protect his

father from her. If he had said so to Mrs Macdonald she would have thought him rude and stupid. How could Sheila harm his father who was thousands of miles away?

Slowly he led the way upstairs.

When they were out of earshot of Mrs Macdonald Sheila whispered, mockingly: 'Why don't you want me to see it?'

He turned on her. 'Because I think you'll bring him bad luck.'

She laughed. 'How could I do that? Do you think I'm a witch?' She made a witch-like face.

In his room she stood looking round. She gave Pegasus an amused sneer, as if all it was was a child's toy. He remembered how reverently Davy Moore had sat on it. He felt Davy's presence in the room, helping to protect him and his father.

She stared at the portrait.

He remembered his mother crying once, 'What is it you want, Hugh? It's not me and it's not Matthew, so what is it?'

Matthew, though he was only six at the time, could have told her. His father wanted to become a famous painter.

That desperate ambition was in his eyes, in the portrait.

'He doesn't look like your father,' said Sheila. 'Your mother looks like your mother but he doesn't look like your father.'

'He's got fair hair.'

'Like me?' She laughed. 'Can I see his studio?'

'All right.'

They went up the steep stairs.

'If this was my house,' she said, 'I'd live up here.'

She was delighted with the studio. 'It's so bright. You feel far away from everybody. Did you know I often go out at night and wander about the town? At one o'clock, when the streets are empty. I've met hedgehogs.'

'Does your father let you?'

'He doesn't know. May I look at the paintings?'

Seeing the paintings through her eyes, Matthew felt that he was seeing his father through her eyes. It was a strange feeling.

'He likes bright colours,' she said.

'Yes.'

'He doesn't like people very much. Neither do I. I wish I had met him.'

It was true his father hadn't liked many people. Sometimes Matthew had not been sure he liked *him*.

'He likes making them ugly and mean-looking, doesn't he? But then so they are ugly and mean-looking.'

'Is Mrs Macdonald ugly and mean-looking?'

She laughed. 'Maybe there are exceptions.'

But when they went into the kitchen Mrs Macdonald said something that though meant to be a kindness showed her for a few moments to be ugly and mean-looking. 'Matthew, why don't you show Sheila the nest?'

He had discovered it three days ago. It was a hedge-sparrow's, with six eggs. It was well hidden in the big rowan tree in the back garden. He thought of it as being under his protection.

He did not want Sheila to see it, but he was too cowardly to give the true reason. 'It's not fair to disturb the birds.'

'It'd be only for a minute or two. I'm sure Sheila would like to see it.'

'Yes, I would.'

He almost blurted out the truth, that he was afraid she would do some harm to the nest. Mrs Macdonald would have thought he was being jealous and childish.

Mrs Macdonald led the way out of the back door into the garden. She went to the shed to get out the stepladder. 'You've got to be careful, Sheila. The ground's not even.'

One of the birds suddenly flew out of the tree.

'You see, we've disturbed it,' said Matthew.

'It'll be back. You go first, Matthew. Show Sheila where it is.'

He went up the ladder unwillingly. He felt that he was acting as Sheila's accomplice. She was staring up him with an odious, gleeful smile.

He parted the twigs and leaves. There was the nest, there were the eggs. He had never seen anything more innocent.

'Are the eggs hatched yet?' asked Mrs Macdonald.

'No.'

'Well, come down and let Sheila have a look.'

Just then they heard the telephone ringing in the house. Mrs Macdonald hurried off to answer it.

Matthew wanted to shout after her not to go. He needed a witness to make sure Sheila did nothing to harm the nest.

Sheila went up the ladder. It shoogled, but she did not mind. She had no fear, because she had no conscience.

Looking up, with the sun in his eyes, he did not see clearly what happened. Sheila seemed to raise her fist and bring it down like a hammer on the nest. Yolk and bits of shell clung to her hand. She laughed gleefully, or so he thought.

She was to claim that, fearful of falling, she had put out her hand and grabbed. Unfortunately she had struck the nest, smashing the eggs. What he had thought laughter was, she said, her cry of regret at her clumsiness.

Mrs Macdonald came out. 'What's happened?'

'She's smashed all the eggs,' said Matthew.

'It was an accident, Mrs Macdonald. I felt I was going to fall so I just grabbed at anything. I struck the nest. I'm so sorry.'

'It wasn't an accident,' he said.

Mrs Macdonald was horrified. 'Are you saying it was done deliberately?'

'Yes.'

'Matthew Sowglass, do you know something? At times you remind me of your Aunt Fiona. Apologise to Sheila.'

'He doesn't have to,' said Sheila. 'He's upset. He doesn't know what he's saying.'

'It's good of you to say so. Well, you'd better go in and wash your hand. It's not the end of the world. It's just a birds' nest.'

It wasn't just that, thought Matthew. It was another instance of evil winning.

Three

He had made up his mind to keep away from Sheila, and at school he managed it, but on Sunday there she was in church, wearing a hat and looking very respectful. She was accompanied by her father, or so he took the small slim bald man to be. His first thought was that Mr Burnside would be easy to push overboard from a tossing sailing-boat, his second that if he was to stand up in the midst of all those godly citizens and accuse her of having that intention every one of them would be horrified. The most charitable ones would think that his mother's death and his father's deserting of him must have deranged his mind; others that he was insanely and pathetically jealous of Sheila who, like him, had lost her mother, but who, unlike him, was bearing it with Christian courage and acceptance.

The majority were elderly ladies, in hats, the kind she had called ugly and useless. Yet there they were, smiling approval at her. If all children were like her, said their smiles, what a blessed place Lunderston would be.

Mrs Macdonald too was deceived. She gave Sheila a wave and was very pleased to get a happy wave in return.

If Sheila was under the Devil's instruction and protection, as Matthew was convinced, it proved, did it not, that the Devil, even there in the church, God's house, was smarter than God? Why was he, one of God's chosen, unable to join in the hymn-singing while she did it so joyously? It was as if she, not he, was one of the Chosen. But surely God would never choose someone so wicked. Matthew had killed the beetle or had tried to kill it, but it had become alive again and to his great relief had crept away unhurt though the grass. Even now, a long time afterwards, he still felt that relief.

If she was in the Devil's power, if she had to do whatever the Devil ordered her to do, should she not be pitied, and not condemned?

The Devil, his grandfather had told him, could assume any appearance he wished. Was he present in the church? In whose body was he hiding? In the old minister's? That was the kind of mischief the Devil loved.

In the church car park Sheila came up to him and Mrs Macdonald, holding her hat in her hand. Her father was with her, wearing his hat. He lifted it to Mrs Macdonald. Matthew noticed how exceptionally clean he was. He seemed a very pernickety man. Perhaps because of his occupation, which brought him into contact with criminals, petty ones mostly, he was determined to be extra-correct in everything he said or did. It should have been impossible to imagine him killing his wife, but somehow it wasn't. He would have done it very efficiently, washing off every speck of blood. The way he held his Bible close to his heart, seemed sinister. Other men had left theirs in the church.

'So you're Matthew,' he said. He did not smile. 'Sheila's told me about you. Thank you for helping her to feel at home in Lunderston.'

'She'll soon make friends,' said Mrs Macdonald. 'She's so outgoing. Matthew's the very opposite. He's much too re-served. She's going to be good for him.'

'I'm going for a cycle run this afternoon to the old castle,' said Sheila. 'Would you like to come with me, Matthew? Have you got a bike?'

'He's got a very good bike,' said Mrs Macdonald.

'The tyres are flat,' he muttered.

'We'll blow them up,' said Sheila.

'One's got a puncture.'

'We'll soon mend it.'

'It'll do you good, Matthew,' said Mrs Macdonald. 'What time will you come for him, Sheila?'

'Would two o'clock suit?'

'He'll be ready by then. When you come back we'll have tea at our place. That's if your father doesn't mind.'

'Not at all,' said Mr Burnside, again without a smile. 'Sheila was telling me you make wonderful pancakes.'

Mrs Macdonald laughed. 'I'll see that she takes some home for you.'

'Thank you.' He lifted his hat again and then he and Sheila made for their car, a white Volvo.

Was it possible, Matthew wondered, that a man who liked pancakes could have murdered his wife?

Matthew and Mrs Macdonald went to her Mini.

'He seems a nice man,' she said. 'A bit starchy, maybe.'

'What's starchy?'

'Stiff. I couldn't imagine him laughing at anything.'

In the car, on their way home, Matthew said, 'Mrs Macdonald, do you believe in the Devil?'

She couldn't help laughing, but she cut it short. This was the kind of question he was liable to ask, in that earnest way of his. Though it ought not to be encouraged she felt obliged to give as reasonable an answer as she could. In the present case perhaps it wasn't such an odd question. After all, they had just come out of church.

'Well, I don't believe in a black slippery creature with horns and a long tail.'

'But he is black and he's got horns and a long tail. My grandfather saw him once. He was trying to get into the church but he couldn't. God kept him out. Sparks were flying from his teeth. There was a terrible smell off him.'

'I think your grandfather likes to let his imagination run away with him.'

'He showed me the scratches the Devil made on the church door with his claws.'

'What nonsense. The Devil's the badness in folks' minds.'

'Who puts the badness in folks' minds?'

It was no use looking for a reasonable answer to that. There wasn't one.

'I saw him once.'

Better, she thought, to humour the child. This was a phase he was going through. No doubt it was connected with his mother's death and his father's absence.

'Where was this? In the Hebrides?'

She had never been there herself but she knew it was full of superstitions.

'No. In my room. He was sitting on Pegasus.'

Grimly, she went on humouring him. 'Was it night-time?'

'Yes.'

'Was the moon shining in? It could have been a trick of the moonlight.'

'Maybe, but I don't think so.'

'When was this?'

'A wee while ago.'

'After you got that letter from your Aunt Fiona?'

'I think so.'

It had contained neither pity nor love, that letter.

'There was a funny smell.'

Coming no doubt from a mess in a corner made by Lucy. On wet nights the old cat didn't fancy going out to do her business.

64

'Sheila Burnside told me that her father killed her mother, and she was going to kill her father.'

'Good heavens, Matthew, do you know what you're saying?'

'Yes. That's what she told me.'

Mrs Macdonald had to believe him. He wasn't a liar. In fact she had often been touched by his steadfast telling of the truth. Nor was he malicious. She had never known him try to get anyone into trouble. Sheila must have been making fun of him, because he was so serious. She had meant it as a joke. Some joke, though.

Four

When Sheila arrived, ringing her bicycle bell cheerfully to let them know she was there, Mrs Macdonald found herself looking with absurd suspicion at the pleasant well-turned-out girl in the red shorts and top to match, and with her long fair hair tied with a red ribbon. She couldn't help it. A girl who, even as a joke, had said that her father had killed her mother and she was going to kill him in revenge, was, to say the least, very unusual. Minutes later when Sheila took over the mending of the puncture she did it with an assurance and self-confidence that Mrs Macdonald found uncanny. It was stupid, terribly stupid, as Mrs Macdonald herself acknowledged, to imagine this affable girl, this child really, being similarly efficient with a knife or axe, but for a dreadful moment or two Mrs Macdonald could not stop herself imagining it.

'Take care,' she cried, as she waved them off.

The danger she felt Matthew might be in wasn't that of collision with a car or a fall off his bicycle. She couldn't have said what kind of danger it was.

When she went back into the house Lucy was in the hall, mewing anxiously, as if she too was apprehensive.

'Don't be daft, Bella Macdonald,' she told herself. 'All the beast wants is food.'

A minute after leaving the house Sheila stopped.

'What's the matter?' he asked.

'I've got an idea. Why don't we pay Miss Johnston a visit?'

It seemed a kind, a Christian idea. Miss Johnston had refused to go into hospital. The nurse looking after her might not be on duty on Sunday afternoon. So the old woman would be alone.

'I don't think we should,' he said.

'Why not?'

He couldn't say it was because he didn't trust her. 'She's too ill. Maybe she's in pain. We shouldn't disturb her.'

'If she's in pain we would take her mind off it. She'll be glad to see you. Weren't you one of her pets?'

'She never had pets.'

'We could take flowers.'

'The shops are shut.'

'We'll get them out of gardens.'

'That would be stealing.'

'In a good cause.' Sheila laughed and cycled off.

He should have turned and returned home, but he cycled after her. He might have to stop Sheila from doing Miss Johnston harm.

Miss Johnston's cottage was in a cul-de-sac, with some other cottages. They all had flowers and bushes in their gardens. It was so quiet and peaceful that birds could be heard singing. Perhaps, thought Matthew, Miss Johnston was listening to them.

'Maybe she's asleep,' he said. 'Mrs Macdonald said people with cancer have to be given drugs to make them sleep. I think we should go.'

'You're an awful coward.'

They had all said he was very brave when his mother had died and his father had gone away. But that had been different. No one else was being hurt except himself.

Sheila slipped through a gate and began to grab some flowers.

No one shouted at her. The people would be in their living-rooms, watching television, at the back of the houses.

She soon came back with a handful of marigolds and gowans. 'They're not worth much,' she said, 'but they'll do.'

She wheeled her bicycle along to Miss Johnston's gate.

He followed, unwillingly. The curtains were drawn in Miss Johnston's cottage. Perhaps she was already dead. He felt a great pity for her. She hadn't been liked but she had never wanted to be liked. That meant she must have been very unhappy. He wished that he could do something now to help her, but he couldn't, he was just a child, and though he was one of God's chosen that didn't mean he had magical powers. He had not been able to keep his mother from dying.

Sheila led the way up the path to the front door.

There were dandelions growing amidst the gravel. If Miss Johnston had been well she'd have dug them up. You had to dig dandelions up because they had such a long root.

He was sure Sheila's father didn't let weeds grow on his path.

There was a bell button. Sheila pressed it, without mercy.

They heard the bell ring inside the house. It seemed to Matthew a sad sound. The singing of the birds sounded sad too.

No one came to the door.

'Maybe she's in bed,' he whispered.

'Don't you hope she's in pain?'

He was shocked.

'She deserves it, doesn't she? I bet Davy Moore thinks so.'

He shook his head. Perhaps Miss Johnston had been cruel to Davy, but Davy would never be cruel in return. He would want to take away her pain. He always forgave.

There was someone on the other side of the door.

Slowly it opened.

Matthew wouldn't have recognised this old white-haired gaunt-faced woman as his former teacher. Nor would he have recognised the voice as hers. It was a painful croak.

'What is it? What do you want?'

'We've come to see you,' said Sheila, cheerfully. 'We've brought you flowers.'

Matthew's voice was hoarse too. 'I'm Matthew Sowglass. Are you all right, Miss Johnston?'

She smiled; well, she looked as if she was trying to smile. There was a smell of medicines off her.

'Has you father come home yet?'

He was amazed that she remembered about his father.

'No, not yet.'

'I'm Sheila Burnside,' said Sheila. 'Can we come in?'

'No, we don't want to,' said Matthew. 'Miss Johnston's tired.'

'Thank you, Matthew. Yes, I'm tired. Thank you for coming. I'm sorry.'

Before Sheila could stop her she closed the door.

Immediately Sheila pressed the bell button.

Matthew seized her hand and pulled it away.

She was furious with him. 'Do you know what you are? You're a fucking hypocrite. Who was it wrote on the blackboard that she was a cunt?'

He hadn't known then that Miss Johnston was ill, but it was no excuse.

Sheila threw away the flowers, pushed him aside, and strode down the path to the gate.

Suddenly she was walking slowly and sadly. Miss Johnston's neighbour, a pink-faced white-haired old woman, was standing at the gate.

'I should have warned you, my dear,' she said. 'The poor soul doesn't want visitors. Were you pupils of hers?'

Sheila's voice trembled. There were tears in her eyes. 'Yes. It's awful her being alone when she's dying.'

'Yes, it is, but it's what she wants. She's always been strange. It was difficult to get to know her. Didn't I see you in church this morning, dear?'

'Yes. I was with my father. He's the new Sheriff Clerk. My name's Burnside, Sheila Burnside.'

The old woman was impressed by that evidence of respectableness. 'And you're Matthew Sowglass?'

'Yes.' He hated those tears in Sheila's eyes. They were so false they made everything else false, even the birds singing.

'Goodbye.' Sheila mounted her bicycle and rode away.

Matthew came after her.

'Another nosy old cunt,' she said.

He noticed again how careful she was not to say these shocking things to anyone but him. To everyone else she was friendly and respectful.

Why had she chosen him to show the badness in her mind? Perhaps it wasn't him she wanted to shock, but God through him.

He must expose her lies. She would be made harmless then. He would challenge her to tell him how her father had killed her mother.

On their way to the Monument they cycled along the shore, past the Yacht Club. Some members waved to her, not just casual waves but enthusiastic ones. She wasn't just admired, she was also liked. If her father ever fell overboard and was drowned, with her in the boat, it would never occur to anyone that she had pushed him. They would all say it was a dreadful accident. She would be showered with pity, not blame. It wouldn't be easy to get them to see the truth. They would think he was the one with badness in his mind.

The Monument was a tall circular stone column, in the shape of a pencil; indeed it was known locally as the Pencil. It had been erected in commemoration of a battle hundreds of years ago between an invading Viking army and the Scots. Many had been killed and wounded on both sides. It was said the sea and shore were red with blood. Today people with imagination thought they could hear the cries of the combatants. People with no imagination heard gulls and oyster-catchers.

It was a favourite picnic spot, with toilets, benches and tables, litter-baskets, and a car park. Some families were picnicking there that sunny afternoon. They smiled when Sheila went about picking up litter. When a toddler of two or so ran towards her and fell on the grass Sheila picked her up and kissed her knee to make it better. The child's parents looked on with approval. When their little girl grew up they hoped she would be kind and helpful like Sheila.

Matthew felt great unease. He couldn't help feeling doubt. Perhaps he was all wrong about her.

Then, when they were seated on a bench, throwing bits of their sandwiches to the gulls, she remarked, in a casual kind of voice, that once in Glasgow she had killed a little girl, a bit younger than the one whose knee she had kissed better. She had been passing a pram, parked outside a shop on a steep street. Making sure no one was looking, she had released the brake and given the pram a push. It had run off the pavement on to the street. A car had struck it. The baby had been thrown out. Its mother had come rushing out of the shop, screaming like a madwoman. A crowd gathered. They were all sympathetic, but one or two had whispered that it had been very careless not to make sure the brake was properly on. An ambulance came, but it was no use, the baby was dead. There was blood on the street.

'I think I was six at the time.'

Surely it was another of her monstrous lies. What was its purpose? To test him? To see if he was so stupid as to believe her?

'I don't believe you,' he said.

'Do you think I care whether you believe me or not?'

'And I don't believe that your father killed your mother.'
She laughed.

'How did he do it? Did he stab her with a knife?'

'There would have been blood if he had done that. My father's a very tidy man. He put a pillow over her face. She was in bed, asleep.'

'How do you know? Did you see it?'

'Yes, I saw it.'

'Why didn't you try to stop him?'

'I just made up my mind to kill him some day.'

'This is stupid,' he said, but he felt afraid.

If he continued to be her companion, or her friend as people might think, and if she kept telling him terrible lies like these, he might lose his mind. He remembered the little girl Veronica who lived near Davy Moore and who, as Davy had said, wasn't 'wice', meaning that she was weak in the head. He might become like that himself if he had to listen to Sheila's lies.

For they were lies, weren't they?

Five

One morning, two days before the summer holidays began, Matthew arrived at school to find great excitement in the boys' playground. A crowd surrounded two boys, Jackie McDade and Gordon Mackie. They were in Matthew's class. They lived in the Glebe, beside Davy Moore.

Usually they were never noticed, for they were very ordinary and were content to be, but that morning they looked very self-important. Though they seemed to be saying something serious, they couldn't help little bursts of self-congratulary laughter.

'What's up?' Matthew asked Tommy Melville, another boy in his class.

'They're saying Davy Moore's been killed.'

'Killed? Was it an accident?'

'Naw. They're saying he's been murdered.'

Matthew pushed forward. They made way for him. Since he lived in a villa and his family owned the Gallery and he wore expensive jeans and he was often top of the class, they always showed him deference.

'What's happened, Jackie? What's all the fuss about?'

Jackie readily repeated what he had already said half a dozen times and those who had heard it half a dozen times again listened keenly. They were confident that Sowglass would get the truth out of Jackie.

'Wee Davy Moore's been found deid, Sowglass. Murdered.'

'Where? Who found him?'

'In Puddock Lane. My uncle Ernie found him. At hauf past six this morning. He was on his way to his work. He works at the pier. He goes through Puddock Lane for a short-cut. He saw what he thought was a bundle of rags, but when he looked closer he saw it was a body, a deid body. He turned it ower and it was wee Davy. He got bluid on his hauns, my uncle did. He ran a' the way tae the polis station. At first they wouldnae believe him but he telt them he wasnae likely tae be drunk at hauf past six in the morning. He was seek in the polis station. He was too seek to go tae his work.'

There was a silence.

'Were they sure it was Davy?' asked Matthew.

Like the others he wasn't yet aware of the horror he felt.

'Aye, it was Davy a' right. His mither identified him.'

They stared at one another fearfully. They were beginning to feel the horror.

'But everybody liked wee Davy,' one said.

'Miss Johnston didnae,' said Gordon Mackie.

They shook their heads. Being sarcastic about Davy's bad scholarship was a different thing altogether from bashing his head in with a brick.

'That big lassie Burnside didnae like him either,' said Sid Fulton. 'she clyped on him.'

But Sid was a stupid fellow and that was the kind of stupid thing a stupid fellow would say.

Matthew remembered Sheila saying that she roamed about the empty streets at dead of night. She had seen hedgehogs.

But the one thing he mustn't do was tell her lies for her, before she told them herself.

'Who dae *you* think did it, Sowglass?' asked Tommy Melville.

They waited for his answer. They were often impressed by

his knowledge. He knew lots of things they didn't. He read encyclopedias.

This time, though, he was as ignorant as they.

'My father said it could hae been somebody escaped frae Laudermuir,' said Gordon Mackie.

Laudermuir was where dangerous lunatics were kept.

They nodded. It was the kind of thing a madman would do.

'It must have happened late last night,' said Matthew.

'Davy was often oot late,' said Jackie. 'Last night he was at Paddy McGuire's hoose looking at horror videos.'

'Paddy's a Pape,' someone said.

'That doesnae mean he's a murderer,' said another.

They nodded, but they weren't absolutely sure. Ancient memories stirred in them.

'It couldnae hae been tae rob him,' said stupid Sid Fulton. 'Davy wouldnae hae onything valuable on him.'

It occurred to some, those who stood by quietly and listened to grown-ups, that terrible things could have been done to poor Davy.

Then, half an hour late, the bell rang, commanding them to line up and be marched into the school.

Miss McLean, whose duty it was for she had taken Miss Johnston's place, wasn't as brisk and sure of herself this morning. She put her whistle to her mouth but forgot to blow it. She checked no one for talking or slouching.

'Dae you think they'll close the school for the day?' asked Tommy Nelville.

'They might,' said Matthew.

'If they dae I ken whaur I'm going. Puddock Lane.'

'The police will have it cordoned off,' said Matthew.

'It will be in a' the papers. Lunderston will be famous.'

The boys were in the classroom first. When the girls came in it was obvious they had heard the news. Some had been crying.

Only Matthew noticed that Sheila Burnside was absent.

Miss McLean then came in and, to everyone's indignation, set them some sums to do. Had she forgotten the holidays were only two days away? Worse still, had she forgotten about Davy Moore? She certainly had forgotten to call the roll.

They were all staring at Davy's empty seat.

Miss McLean's voice was angrier than she felt. 'You will have heard about what has happened to your classmate, David Moore. It's a terrible thing but it would be better if you tried not to think about it. In the meantime concentrate on your arithmetic.'

She then remembered she hadn't marked the register. There were only two absentees, Davy Moore and Sheila Burnside.

'Does anyone know what's the matter with Sheila?'

No one did and no one cared. Except Matthew.

If, lying and boasting as usual, she claimed to have killed Davy what should he do? What could he do?

An hour or so later, when they had moved on to parsing and analysis, word came that the school was to be dismissed for the day. Pupils were advised not to hang about but to go straight home.

Nevertheless, many did hang about in the playgrounds, talking. It was thought strange that Davy, after watching horror videos for hours, had walked home alone, at midnight. But then, in June, it was never really dark, and vampires didn't exist, did they? And besides Lunderston was a place where it was safe to be out at night. At least it had been yesterday, it wasn't now and wouldn't be again, for a long time.

Six

M ost of the boys set out for Puddock Lane, but Matthew drifted off in the opposite direction, towards Ailsa Park, the new residential area of smart expensive bungalows where Sheila lived. He walked slowly. He hadn't made up his mind to go to her house. What could he say to her? If she hadn't heard about Davy he could tell her, but he might then have to listen to her worst lie yet.

He rested on a bench overlooking the town. In the bright sunshine Lunderston looked splendid, but also sinister. Yonder was the ferry, its funnels red as rowanberries, crossing to the island. Usually it lifted his heart to see it sailing so staunchly, but not today. Beyond the island were the mountains of Arran. He made out the Sleeping Warrior. People with no imagination could never see how the outline of the peaks against the sky resembled a helmeted warrior, lying on his back, asleep, but Matthew always saw it. Today, though, the Warrior was not sleeping, he was dead. There, close to the cemetery, was the hospital. In its mortuary Davy's body would be lying under a white sheet. But what about his soul, the part that never died, as the minister often said? Was it still in the body, getting ready to leave? Or was it already yonder in the blue sky, high as an eagle, on its journey to some far-off unimaginable place, where it would be greeted by his granny's soul?

A black and white dog limped past, panting. Its red tongue hung out. It had no collar. It looked hungry. It gave him a quick glance: he was no use to it. He wouldn't feed it or take it home with him and look after it. He would have liked to, but how could he? Mrs Macdonald wouldn't have allowed it, and Lucy would have been jealous.

At last he got up and went on. He came upon the house unexpectedly. There was a name plate attached to the gate: Goatfell View.

It was the tidiest bungalow in that district of tidy bunga-lows. There wasn't a single blade of grass amidst the gravel on the path. There were lots of roses in the front garden, but none of their petals seem to have fallen, as rose petals did. Did Mr Burnside gather them up as soon as they fell? What he couldn't do, though probably he would want to, was keep out the bees. Matthew counted six, and one butterfly, a red admiral. He felt a great fondness for these remote small creatures, just as he had done for the stray dog. He thought of his father thousands of miles away, and of his mother still further. Tears threatened to come into his eyes. He stifled them with his knuckle. He had vowed never to let anyone see him weep, not even Mrs Macdonald, and especially not Sheila.

He was about to turn away when the front door opened, and there she was, staring at him. She was dressed in blue jeans and white blouse. Her right hand was bandaged. She looked pale and unwell.

She came out and walked, with strange menace, towards him as if minded to strike him. But suddenly she pressed her bandaged hand against her breast.

'What do you want?' she asked. 'What are you doing here?'

'You weren't at school. I wondered what was wrong.'

She sneered. 'So you've come to spy on me?'

What had she done that she was afraid would be found out?

'Have you heard the news? Did your father tell you?'

'Tell me what? What news?'

'Davy Moore's dead. He was killed, murdered. Last night. In Puddock Lane. His head was bashed in with a brick.'

'A brick? Are you sure it wasn't a half brick? A whole brick would be hard to hold, unless you had a very big hand.'

He remembered how with her small hand she had smashed the eggs in the nest.

Why was her hand bandaged? A brick had sharp edges.

'Where's Puddock Lane?' she asked.

'It's between Bruce Street and Victoria Road. People use it as a short-cut.'

'Why have you come to tell me? If you think I'm going to be sorry for that little fool you're mistaken.'

'What's the matter with your hand?'

'I fell off my bike.'

She was the most skilful and the safest cyclist he knew.

She turned then and went back towards the house. She went straight in and shut the door.

Seven

As he made his way home he felt depressed. Nothing he saw cheered him up. An old man mowing his small lawn, a robin on a bush, a baby in a pram, gulls in the sky, sights that yesterday would have reassured him, today added to his depression. His father would die in the distant country and Matthew would never see him again; just as he would never see his mother again.

Mrs Macdonald was ironing in the kitchen. She hurried into the hall to greet him. She had heard the news on the radio.

'Isn't it awful?' she cried. 'Such an inoffensive little boy. Did the school close early?'

'Yes.'

'I thought it would. My God, what's the world coming to? Who'd have thought such a thing could happen in Lunderston?'

As he went into the kitchen Lucy trotted after him. He bent and patted her. He remembered she hadn't let Davy pat her.

Mrs Macdonald resumed her ironing. 'Sheila Burnside has just phoned. Poor girl, she had just heard the news. She was crying.'

'Why? She didn't like Davy.'

'That's not a nice thing to say, Matthew.'

'It's true.'

'I don't think you understand her, Matthew. You've got to remember that she's lost her mother, just like you.'

Not like me, he could have said. It was cancer killed my mother. It was Sheila's father who killed Sheila's mother. Or so Sheila told me.

But he didn't want to talk about Sheila. 'Was there any mail today?'

He asked every day and every day she had to give him the same dismal answer. At such times she felt very angry with his father.

'Just the usual junk.'

There was silence then. Mrs Macdonald went on ironing, Lucy washed her face, and Matthew thought about his father.

'When I grow up,' he said,' if my father hasn't come home by then, I'll go and look for him.'

'Would you know where to look?'

'Isn't he in that town in Mexico? Villahermosa.' The lawyer still sent money to the address there.

'Why doesn't he write?'

He had never asked that before, but no doubt the question was in his mind all the time.

'I don't know, son. I really don't know.'

'I've written but he didn't reply.'

The lawyer had sent on letters. There had been no replies.

She almost said, bitterly, Because he's selfish and callous. But the boy would have been hurt, and besides, she did not remember Sowglass as selfish and callous.

'Perhaps he's ill.'

Debilitating long-lasting diseases could be picked up in tropical countries.

'But probably he's just too busy with his painting.'

'He could send postcards.'

'People get out of the habit of writing, Matthew. Days go

by. They say, I'll write tomorrow, but they don't, and they don't the next day either.'

'Years go by,' he said.

She almost wept.

'I think he doesn't want me, because my mother died.'

'How could he blame you for that?'

'I didn't say he blamed me. He just doesn't want me. He doesn't want anyone.'

'But you're his son. He should want you, all the more that your mother's gone.'

The telephone rang in the hall.

'I'll answer it,' he said.

He didn't think it would be Sheila, he hoped it wasn't, but it was.

'I just wanted to tell you that when I said I hurt my hand falling off my bike it wasn't true.'

She wanted him to ask how she had hurt it but he refused.

'Have you ever held a half brick in your hand?' she asked. 'It's quite heavy and it's got sharp edges.'

He still said nothing.

'I don't think you could get fingerprints on a brick. It's too rough.' She laughed. 'They'll never get whoever did it. Unless someone confesses. Do you think someone will confess? Of course nobody's really to blame. Wasn't everything arranged thousands of years ago, millions of years ago, when the world began. Wasn't that what your grandfather told you? You'd have to blame God, wouldn't you, for He was the one who arranged it.'

His grandfather was gravely ill. There had been a letter from Aunt Fiona, saying that Matthew might want to see him before he died, and saying too that his grandfather didn't want to see him.

Malignant bitch, Mrs Macdonald had muttered.

'I'll be seeing you,' said Sheila. 'Cheerio.'

He went back into the kitchen.

'Was it Sheila?' asked Mrs Macdonald.

'Yes.'

'What did she want?'

'Nothing.'

'Will you be seeing a lot of her during the holidays?'

'I don't know.'

'I don't think you should. I've changed my mind about her. I don't think she's such a good influence. Maybe you should go and see your grandfather. They tell me it's beautiful there in summer.'

He remembered the machair with its flowers, bees, and skylarks. He remembered the little green beetle. He remembered his grandfather's resentful, defeated face.

'I don't want to,' he said.

'He *is* your grandfather.'

'He hates my father.'

It seemed to Mrs Macdonald that it had been Matthew's mother the implacable old man had hated.

'Maybe one of your other aunts will invite you.'

'I wouldn't go. Excuse me, please.'

He got up and went out. She heard him trudging slowly up the stairs.

She felt great anxiety. She had thought that she was making a good enough job of bringing him up, but now she was doubtful. He had never been an outgoing merry-minded child, like poor Davy Moore. Since his mother's death and his father's abandoning of him he had become more and more withdrawn and unhappy, and she had not been able to prevent it. Who, though, could have? His father? Maybe. But his father was at the other end of the earth and was determined to stay there.

Eight

O n his way to school, that last day before the holidays, Matthew passed Mr Marshall's newsagent's shop. Outside it were two large placards, one for the *Herald* and the other for the *Chronicle*, the newspaper that Mrs Macdonald read: she liked its horoscopes. Both placards proclaimed, in big black letters: Lunderston Boy Murdered. There would be placards like these outside newsagents all over Scotland. Lunderston had become famous. People would look it up on the map.

Two grey-haired women, coming out of the shop, one with a copy of the *Chronicle* in her hand, caught sight of him, a boy walking by himself in the murderous streets.

'You tak care, son,' said one of them. 'God kens wha's aboot these days.' And she stared at the passers-by, with frowning suspicion.

He had a funny feeling that everybody he saw felt and looked more important than they had done yesterday. Then Davy Moore, happy and carefree, hadn't mattered; it had been of no consequence to have known him. Today, Davy, with his head bashed in and with his photograph in the newspapers, was different. People would boast that they had known him.

In the school playground Matthew found his classmates talking about Davy in shrill excited voices. Their faces gloated.

They had known things about Davy that other people didn't. They had known he was a dunce, who couldn't spell. They had known he had once been arrested for shoplifting. So, now that he was a celebrity, like a football player or pop star, they felt that they were entitled to a share of his fame. Some even envied him.

When Matthew went into the classroom he looked to see if Sheila was among the girls. He wanted to see if her hand was still bandaged. She wasn't there, but then, quite a number were absent, this being the last day and there would be no lessons, and also some parents wouldn't have allowed their children out unattended, while that evil monster was still loose.

It was the custom on that last morning for the whole school to be marched to St Cuthbert's church for a service. It was also the custom for many boys to skip it, but none skipped it this morning. They were all eager to hear what the old minister would say about the murder. He always said that Jesus Christ loved children and protected them. Would he say it this time?

What he did say, at the beginning, surprising them all, was that Miss Johnston the teacher had died. They wondered at the coincidence. Just as the blows with the brick were killing Davy cancer had killed her. Did that mean they had arrived in heaven together? Or maybe in hell?

The minister said nothing about Jesus Christ loving little children. In fact he said nothing at all about Davy. Evidently he and Mr Buchanan the headmaster had decided it would be better not to.

After the service, which was very short, a group of Davy's classmates conferred in the church grounds. Having seen many murder stories on television they knew how investigations were conducted. Had Davy been sexually assaulted? This had to be explained to one or two simpletons who didn't understand. Had there been fragments of skin under Davy's nails that he had torn from the murderer's face? Had the murderer left any clues at the scene, such as bloodstains or footprints?

They turned to Matthew, who hadn't spoken.

'Whit dae you think, Sowglass?'

'Dae you think they'll catch who did it?'

'If it was somebody Davy knew,' he said, 'they'll find him, but if he was a stranger I don't think they'll find him.'

He was thinking: had Davy known Sheila? Not really.

'That's whit my faither said,' said a boy. 'He said maist murders are done by relatives. If a wife's murdered it's nearly always her man that did it; and the ither way roon'.'

'Whit wad onybody want to kill him for?' asked another. 'He had nothing worth stealing. It must hae been a madman.'

'That's right,' they agreed. 'A madman doesnae need a motive. Does he, Sowglass?'

But, thought Matthew, evil itself was a motive.

He still believed in angels but was no longer sure that they were always beneficent.

Nine

No funerals could have been more different. Miss Johnston's was on Wednesday, a day, as it happened, of rain, lightning and thunder, the kind of day indeed that she would have wished. It was easy to imagine her in the coffin smiling grimly. In her will she had asked to be cremated. That meant her remains had to be conveyed through the storm to Gantock, fifteen miles away. Perhaps if it had been a warm welcoming sunny day a few of her former pupils might have made the journey, though the announcement in the *Gazette* had stressed the funeral was to be private and even in death she demanded obedience. There was to be no minister. This hurt and disappointed old Mr Henderson who for thirty years had been under the impression that he was her pastor whose duty it should have been to usher her into God's celestial fold. That she had once told him she didn't believe in God wouldn't have mattered. As a consequence there was no eulogy, as the Americans called it. This was just as well, for who, without a lot of humbug, could have praised her?

There was, though, one rather odd connection between the two funerals. It didn't come out until months later when the terms of Miss Johnston's will became known. She left all her money, a goodly sum, to Lunderston Primary School, except for a bequest of 500 pounds to David Moore, of Laverock Terrace.

There was to be much debate in the town as to who should get the money now that poor Davy himself was dead. Some thought it should go to his family, others that the school should have it. In the end lawyers got most of it.

But all that was in the future.

Davy's funeral took place on Friday, two days after the teacher's. To no one's surprise, for Lunderston's weather was very changeable, it turned out to be a day of sunshine and blue skies. It was a proper funeral, a burial not a burning, and hundreds attended. Not only was old Mr Henderson of St Cuthbert's present, so too were three other ministers, the Baptist, the Pentecostal, and, controversially, the Catholic. There was a procession, from the Glebe to the cemetery, with an Orange Lodge band from Glasgow playing mournful but rather strident music. Mr Moore, it seemed, was a member of the Lunderston Lodge and Davy had been a fanatical Rangers supporter. Members of various Lodges were there, with sashes and black bowlers. It was thought that Mrs Moore didn't approve but she kept quiet about it. It was generally agreed that religious prejudice could have had nothing to do with the murder, though there were bound to be a few who weren't convinced that the Pope's crafty and bloody hand wasn't in it somewhere.

Present also were detectives, in the hope that the murderer showed up and gave himself away; policemen, to keep order; reporters, TV camera men; teachers who hadn't yet set off for their holidays; and classmates of Davy's, among them Matthew Sowglass. Unlike them he had been invited.

There had been a telephone call from Mrs Moore. She spoke to Mrs Macdonald.

'Jessie Moore here. I'd like the boy to come to the funeral.'

Mrs Macdonald was taken aback. 'Do you mean Matthew?'

'Aye. Davy would have liked him to be there. Will he come?'

Mrs Macdonald wasn't sure. Matthew's attitude to Davy had puzzled her and she knew he hated funerals.

'Just a minute, Mrs Moore, and I'll ask him.'

He was in the front room by the window, reading.

'That's Mrs Moore, Davy's mother, on the phone. She wants you to come to the funeral.'

He didn't answer immediately.

'You don't have to, if you don't want to.'

'It's all right. I'd like to.'

'Will I tell her that?'

'Yes, please.'

She hurried back to the telephone. 'He says he'd like to come. I expect half of Lunderston will be there.'

'No' a' of them welcome. I'd like him to sit in the caur wi' me and Charlie. The rest will be walking.'

Mrs Macdonald thought that Matthew would have preferred to be among the crowd walking but she didn't say so. 'I haven't had a chance, Mrs Moore, to tell you how shocked and sorry I am.'

'He liked you. He said you were kind to him.'

'It was easy to be kind to him. He was such a nice little boy.'

Mrs Macdonald was in tears but she felt that the woman she was talking to was dry-eyed.

She went back to the front room. She had had what she thought was a brainwave.

'You could wear your kilt.'

He had worn it at his mother's funeral. Mrs Macdonald had thought he looked like a little Highland prince.

'It's too wee,' he said.

She had often noticed that children were less sentimental and romantic than adults.

Ten

O n Friday morning – the funeral was at two – he had a telephone call from Sheila.

'Are you going to this stupid funeral?' she asked.

He should have said nothing but he couldn't resist saying, dourly, 'It's not stupid.'

'So you're going?'

'Yes.'

'Why? You didn't know him very well. You didn't even like him.'

'I did like him.'

'So why did you invite him to your house only once? Were you afraid he would steal something?'

'No, I wasn't.'

She laughed. 'I should have been specially invited, for if it hadn't been for me there wouldn't be a funeral.'

'You're being stupid.'

She changed the subject. 'No letter from your father yet?'

She liked to torment him about his father.

'You never will. Do you know why? Because he's dead.'

It wasn't the first time she had said that; never when anyone else was present, and never with pity.

90

'But you should be glad. All the money's now yours. The shop. That big house. You know, when I grow up, I think I'll marry you.'

She was laughing again when she put the telephone down.

Eleven

In the big black limousine, with Mr and Mrs Moore, he kept looking out to see if Sheila, in spite of her sneers, was among the crowd, having come to gloat. Daft wee Veronica was beside him. She had demanded to be taken. Mr Moore had muttered; for Christ's sake, no; but Mrs Moore had lifted her in. Her nose kept needing to be wiped.

Mr Moore didn't try to keep back tears. Mrs Moore did. It wasn't because she missed Davy less, but because she missed him more. She was too proud to let people see her suffer. Like Matthew himself.

There were two limousines. Davy's brother Joe was in the other one, with relatives. Matthew was the only outsider, except Veronica and she didn't count. He wondered why he had been invited. He felt like a fraud. Mrs Moore seemed to think he and Davy had been close friends.

She wasn't pleased at the size of the crowd. 'It's a bluidy circus,' she muttered.

'Folk want to show their sympathy,' whined her husband.

'Are you shair they're no enjoying themsels?'

'Don't be bitter, Jessie.'

'We could hae done withoot the band.'

'Davy liked bands.'

Matthew remembered Davy had liked playing the mouth organ.

'I juist cannae believe it,' said Mr Moore, in a burst of anguish and anger. 'I keep thinking this is a dream, a fucking nightmare. If I could get my hauns on the mad cunt that did it I'd tear his hert oot.'

'That's no' language tae use in front o' weans,' said his wife.

He glared gloomily at Veronica. 'She doesnae even ken this is a funeral. Lucky wee cunt.'

'There's the boy.'

Mr Moore then stared at Matthew. 'Sorry, son.'

'It's all right, Mr Moore.'

Suddenly Veronica yelled: 'Whaur's Davy? I cannae see Davy.'

Not even Mrs Moore knew what to say to her.

Mr Moore had a black handbag. She opened it and, rummaging, took out Matthew's compass. 'I believe this is yours, son. Davy said you gave it to him.'

Matthew nodded.

'He treasured it. He'd hae wanted you to have it back.'

Matthew took it and put it in his pocket, gently restraining Veronica who tried to grab it.

'Have you had nae word yet frae your faither?' asked Mrs Moore.

It was common knowledge in Lunderston that his father had deserted him.

'No.'

'Never mind, son. He must hae his reasons. He'll be back one day, you'll see.'

Then, now that they were in the cemetery, past the thronged gate, Mrs Moore got ready to play the part of grieving mother at the graveside. She didn't weep, though.

Listening to Mr Henderson, the minister, or trying to for gulls squawked noisily overhead, Matthew tried to keep out of his mind the possibility that Sheila Burnside, in her midnight wanderings, had met Davy and for no reason except sheer wickedness had attacked him with the brick. Her hand would have been hurt. It would have been covered with blood, hers and Davy's.

It was utterly incredible, it meant that he was letting himself be affected by her ridiculous lies, and yet that awful possibility kept creeping into his mind.

After the ceremony Mrs Moore invited him back to the house for refreshments. 'Sausage rolls and lemonade,' she said.

She was the only person there capable of irony.

When he shyly declined she didn't persist. 'Thanks for coming,' she said. 'You've been a great help to me.'

He didn't understand how he had been a help to her. He had hardly said anything.

When the car stopped outside the close in Laverock Terrace he slipped away, unnoticed.

He did not go straight home but made for the sea-front near the pier. He bought an ice-cream wafer and sat on a bench eating it. Gulls came and eyed him with their yellow eyes, demanding their share. He wondered how they could eat ice cream with those sharp curved beaks. The red spots reminded him of blood.

Were there gulls where his father was, in the far-off country?

Twelve

Like everybody else in the town the police were soon convinced that the murderer must have been mad. No sane person could have killed a happy harmless little boy. A few old-fashioned Lunderstonians secretly thought that Davy had been too young to be allowed out by himself so late, but they didn't say it aloud, except to husbands and close friends. His parents had suffered enough and besides Lunderston had long prided itself on being a town where old ladies weren't afraid to walk home from bingo after dark.

Then, to everybody's relief, the police, during their door-to-door enquiries, found the culprit, or thought they had.

In an isolated cottage by the Balgie Burn, in a jungle of a garden, lived old Mrs Saunders' and her unfortunate, misshapen son Malky. When the police called he was skulking in an outhouse and readily confessed. Now about forty he had been in and out of mental hospitals all his life, but to be fair he had never been thought of as dangerous or violent. Children yelled derision at him and mocked his shambling gait, but he had never been known to retaliate; indeed, he didn't seem to have noticed. When it became known that he had been arrested many were sceptical. True enough, though, weren't there dogs, family pets, that suddenly went mad and savaged children that minutes ago they had been playing with?

One person who resolutely refused to believe that Malky was guilty was Mrs Moore, Davy's mother. Defying the police, she went to Mrs Saunders' cottage to tell her so.

She was soon proved right. Further investigation exonerated Malky, who probably had never known that he had been accused.

Still assuming that the killer must have been a local man the detectives next suspected Rab McCandlish, an elderly kenspeckle curmudgeon who slouched about the town in a long filthy overcoat muttering threats and obscenities. He had once been a normal enough citizen, employed by the council's parks department, but that was before his wife had died twelve years ago. He lived by himself in Wallace Street, where his neighbours kept complaining to the police and the housing department about the filthiness, outside and in, of his house. Social workers had given him up as irredeemable, but really the only thing that could have redeemed Rab was the restoration of his Bella, and that was not possible. God indeed got a good share of the threats. Rab was often seen shaking his fist at churches. With his mumbling misanthropy, his smelly clothes, his bloodshot eyes, and his antipathy to children (he and Bella never had any) he was a likely enough culprit, but alas his neighbours reluctantly supplied him with an alibi. On the night of the murder they had looked in, as they often did, and found him on the floor, blind drunk, with mice scurrying about him.

It became apparent that the killer might not after all have been a local man. In a way this was a relief, but it meant that the mysterious mad stranger – what the hell was he doing in Lunderston that night? – might never be caught.

Thirteen

Though he was now afraid of her he was also afraid for her. His own loneliness would one day be ended when his father came home. He could foresee great happiness. But there was nothing happy in store for Sheila.

What made it worse was that she seemed to be fond of him; though she could only show it by tormenting him and trying to involve him in her insane fantasies. Dimly he realised that she couldn't help it. She did it because it was her nature, and because she was controlled by the Devil. If he could he would have saved her.

Every day during the holidays she came to his house. When Mrs Macdonald was present she pretended to be interested in books, music, jigsaws, birds, flowers, clothes, and even cooking, the kind of things any bright happy girl of eleven would be interested in. It was when Mrs Macdonald wasn't there that she showed what was really in her mind. Then, with her face almost unrecognisable with insane glee and conceit, she would come close and whisper, never actually saying that she had killed Davy or that she intended to kill her father, but hinting it. He resolutely refused to believe her but he could not help feeling involved.

He knew he should report her, but to whom? The police? Her father? Mrs Macdonald? They would all think he was the one with the bad thoughts.

One wet dull day, when he was feeling depressed, he decided to go for a walk in the rain to the cemetery, to visit his mother's grave. He told Mrs Macdonald. She tried to dissuade him: it was too wet, it would just make him more unhappy. But he was determined.

When Sheila arrived at the house, just as he was about to set out, Mrs Macdonald was relieved. She suggested Sheila should go with him.

Dourly he shook his head and muttered that he wanted to go alone. He was told, cheerfully by Sheila, that that was silly, and sternly by Mrs Macdonald, that he was being impolite. He had used to be such an obliging well-mannered little boy. What had happened to him? She knew of course what had happened to him. His mother had died and his father had deserted him.

Mrs Macdonald stood at the front door waving them off. When they came back – they mustn't be long – she would have hot pancakes ready for them. They seemed to her quite beautiful, like brother and sister, Sheila in red and Matthew in yellow. Surely she had been wrong in thinking Sheila wasn't a good influence on him. Sheila was the kind of daughter Mrs Macdonald would have wished, but she wasn't sure any longer that Matthew was the kind of son she would have liked. She loved him, but he was too private, too remote; he had too many secrets.

As they walked along Sheila mischievously tried to take his hand. Peevishly he withdrew it. She laughed.

They passed two ladies who knew her. Their husbands were members of the Yacht Club.

'Good afternoon,' she said, cheerfully.

They peered at her from under their umbrellas. They were charmed. 'Good afternoon, Sheila. Where are you off to?'

'Matthew wants to visit his mother's grave. I'm going with him.'

'That's very kind of you, Sheila.'

They stared with puzzled pity at Matthew. Why did the poor lad want to visit his mother's grave on such a miserable afternoon? It would still be there tomorrow, wouldn't it, and the sun might be shining.

As Sheila and Matthew went on she said, 'Stupid bitches. They don't know anything, do they?'

'Why were you so nice to then, if that's what you think?'

She laughed. 'You've got an awful lot to learn, haven't you?'

They had the cemetery to themselves except for, said Sheila, the dead people, who didn't count.

'Do you know I've been here at midnight and I never saw a ghost?'

There was a robin in a yew bush. Not long ago it would have given him courage, but not now. Nothing did any more.

He stood by his mother's grave. There were withered flowers on it but he did not remove them. He thought of the flowers on the machair where his mother had played as a child. If Sheila hadn't been there he might have wept.

She stood beside him. Rain stotted on their oilskins.

'Are you praying?' she asked.

He shook his head.

'Do you never pray?'

He had used to pray.

'I never pray,' she said, scornfully. 'It's stupid. It's just like talking to yourself.'

His mother had often prayed. He had knelt beside her. He had been very small then.

'I've got something to show you,' said Sheila.

She put her hand into her oilskin pocket and took it out tightly clenched.

Whatever it was in her hand it must be very small.

He felt in his pocket for his compass. He felt reassured. It still had some magic.

'Don't you want to see it?'

He shrugged. He preferred to look at the robin, now perched on a nearby headstone.

'Look.' She opened her hand slowly. On her palm was a button, a small black ordinary button. Mrs Macdonald had a canister full of them.

'Do you see the blood?'

It could have been blood, but it could have been dirt or rust.

'It came off his jerkin.'

It could have come off anyone's jerkin.

He felt then a great longing for his mother and for the places, the beautiful places, where she had spent her childhood. There were photographs in the album at home. She looked bravely happy in them.

'Do you want it, as a keepsake?'

He shook his head.

'What will I do with it?'

Again he shook his head.

'I tell you what I'll do, I'll bury it with him.'

She went off them looking for Davy's grave. It wasn't easy to find, for there was as yet no headstone. She chose one that looked new and knelt by it. She pushed the button into the earth with her finger.

Matthew watched in amazement.

She was now beating the earth with her fist. Did she think it was Davy's face she was punching?

Soon she rose and ran towards the cemetery gate. She passed close to him but did not speak. He had never seen anyone so unhappy and desperate, not even when, after his mother's death, he had looked in the mirror.

Should he have tried to help her? It was too late now. She was gone.

But where could she go to? Not home. She didn't regard

that neat bungalow where her father lived as home. She had no one kind like Mrs Macdonald. She didn't want anyone kind.

He waited another twenty minutes by his mother's grave, but not thinking about her all the time. He thought about his father.

Fourteen

M rs Macdonald was surprised and concerned when he came back without Sheila.

'I thought she was coming back with you.'

'She didn't want to.'

'Why? Did you have a fall-out?'

'No. I don't think she's well.'

'Aye, I've noticed how she turns pale all of a sudden. It could be her age. Her father should take her to see the doctor.'

He sat in the cosy kitchen, sipping milk and eating a pancake.

'Mrs Macdonald, I think I'd like to go to Uist.'

She was astonished. 'Uist?'

'Yes.'

'What on earth for?'

'To see my grandfather and my Aunt Fiona.'

She almost blurted out that the last time they hadn't been very nice to him. But his mother had been alive then.

She tried to smile. 'What's brought this on?' Old fool, she called herself, inwardly. Hasn't he just been to his mother's grave?

She believed in reconciliations. The nicest parts of the romances she read was when the lovers, after numerous

fall-outs caused by foolish misunderstandings, were recon-
ciled, and so the ending was happy.

But this was real life, where grudges and spites and hatreds
were taken to the grave.

'I just thought I'd like to.'

'What has changed your mind?'

He didn't answer. Rightly so. She had no business asking.

'Well, if you're serious would you like me to write to your
Aunt Fiona?'

'Couldn't I just telephone?'

'Of course you could, but I still think I should speak to her
first.'

'All right. Will we speak to her now?'

'Now?'

'Yes.'

He was so calm, she so flustered.

She tidied her hair and put on a fresh apron. The bitter
woman in Uist couldn't see her, but that wasn't the
point.

He stood beside her in the hall, under the stag's head.

They listened to the ringing in the house far away. Mrs
Macdonald felt fearful. The boy could be in for another cruel
rebuff.

Then they heard that curt voice, like a seal's bark, Mrs
Macdonald thought, though she had heard seals barking only
on television.

'Uist 288,' said the voice.

Mrs Macdonald spoke as genteelly as she could. 'Is that
Miss McLure? Miss Fiona McLure?'

'It is. Who are you?'

'I'm Isabel Macdonald, speaking from Lunderston. I look
after your nephew Matthew Sowglass.'

There was a pause. Was this going to be the end of the
conversation?

'What do you want? Is anything wrong? Has his father come back?'

How could the return of the boy's father be something wrong? Surely it was the most right thing that could happen to him.

'No, it's nothing like that. Here's Matthew himself to speak to you.'

He took the telephone. He was so grave, so courteous, and so responsible that Mrs Macdonald felt like crying. If that heartless besom rebuffed him she deserved to go to hell. Mrs Macdonald did not believe in hell but she was sure Aunt Fiona did.

'Good evening, Aunt Fiona,' he said. 'I'm Matthew Sowglass.'

'What do you want, Matthew Sowglass?'

'I would like to come and visit you.'

A pause. Then one merciless word. 'Why?'

'I would like to see my grandfather. Is he still not well?'

'I doubt if he wants to see you.'

Bitch, thought Mrs Macdonald, who had her ear close to the telephone.

'Well, could you ask him, please?'

'He's asleep.'

'Could you ask him when he wakes up?'

'He's in pain when he's awake.'

So had been his daughter in pain, thought Mrs Macdonald, and he had showed her no pity.

'I'm sorry,' said Matthew. 'I've got another reason.'

'And what's that?'

'I want to see the places where my mother played when she was my age.'

Not only was Aunt Fiona taken aback – they heard her gasp – so was Mrs Macdonald.

'If you come here, boy, never mention your mother.'

'I couldn't promise that.'

'Then don't bother to come.'

That was that. Mrs Macdonald could imagine the telephone being slammed down.

'It's incredible,' she said. 'They're supposed to be godly folk. Well, never mind, son. You and me will go to Glasgow and stay with my sister Beatrice. We could visit the Art Galleries.'

There was another gallery in Glasgow where some of his father's paintings were on show. If she could remember the name of it they could go there too.

The telephone rang again.

'If it's Sheila,' he said, 'I don't want to speak to her.'

But it wasn't Sheila, it was Aunt Fiona, as hard-voiced as ever.

'If he's coming he'd better fly. He can afford it. It's a long journey by train and boat. If you put him on the plane in Glasgow he'll be met in Benbecula.'

'Will you meet him yourself?'

'He'll be met.'

'I'll ask him.'

He was standing by her side.

'She thinks you should fly.'

He nodded.

'Somebody will meet you at Benbecula.'

He nodded again. He was too forgiving, she thought.

To his aunt she spoke sternly. 'Miss McLure, you can tell me it's none of my business, but I think it is. His father left him in my care. I don't want him to be hurt. He's suffering enough, from his mother dying and his father deserting him.'

At least Aunt Fiona refrained from saying that those were the two best things that could have happened to him. She was probably thinking it, though.

Fifteen

The stewardess made a fuss of him all the way. He was the perfect passenger, polite, undemanding, appreciative, and interested. She wondered why his father or mother or some other relative wasn't accompanying him, but she was too tactful to ask. Someone was meeting him, he said, with a smile, and though she had other things to attend to when they landed at Benbecula she made sure that there was someone. This turned out to be an elderly taxi-driver called Dugald, wearing a chauffeur's hat. He explained that the boy's aunt, Miss McLure, had sent him. She hadn't been able to come herself, for her father, the boy's grandfather, was very ill.

The stewardess said to Matthew she'd look out for him on his return flight, in a week's time.

It was a typical Hebridean summer's day. There were blinks of sun. The wind blew constantly. Spume from the nearby Atlantic flew through the air. Some splashed on the taxi's windscreen.

On either side of the road were many lochans, their surfaces ruffled by the wind. The whole landscape seemed to be trying to flee somewhere.

'So you're Catriona's boy,' said Dugald.

Matthew was sitting beside him. 'Yes.'

There were swans on one of the lochans. Matthew felt reassured.

'A bonny girl and brave with it. I tell you, the whole island was very sorry to hear she had died so young.'

Matthew didn't know what to say, so he just said, 'Thank you.'

'Are you from Glasgow?'

'No. I live in Lunderston.'

'Lunderston? Was that where the boy was murdered a wee while back?'

'Yes.'

'Did you know him?'

'He was in my class at school.'

'You tell me that now. They haven't caught the villain that did it.'

'No.'

'Is that why they've sent you here, till the danger's past?'

Well, was that why he had come here? Was he keeping out of Sheila's way, because he couldn't get rid of the suspicion that she might be guilty?

'You'll know your grandfather's badly?'

'Yes.'

'If ever there was a man of God it was your grandfather.'

Yes, but he had not been chosen as one of the Elect.

Dugald fell silent then and Matthew had no wish to speak.

In less than half an hour they were in his grandfather's parish. There was the church, standing by itself, with a tin roof and no steeple. Were the scratches still on the door?

'There's a young fellow taking his place,' said Dugald. 'They say he's got no fire in his belly. But I'm from Loch-maddy myself.'

They stopped at the manse door. Matthew noticed that the garden was overrun with weeds.

'When your grandfather was able,' said Dugald, 'this garden grew the best vegetables in all the isles. Mind you, that's maybe not saying very much. We're not enthusiastic gardeners here. Too much wind. Too many sheep. Too many rabbits. Too much salt in the air.'

As he got out of the taxi Matthew tasted salt on his lips.

Aunt Fiona must have been watching from a window because the front foor opened and there she was, wearing a long tweed skirt in a dark tartan and a black cardigan. Her hair was whiter than he remembered. He got ready to smile but she didn't so he didn't either.

Ignoring him she spoke to Dugald, in Gaelic.

Matthew remembered that his mother had spoken Gaelic. She had tried to teach him.

Dugald drove away. He gave Matthew a wave.

Aunt Fiona stood staring at him. Still she did not smile. Neither therefore did he.

'You've brought just the one case?'

'Yes.'

'Is it heavy?'

'Not very.'

They had to speak loudly because of the wind. He could hear the sea crashing on to the sand. He had once thought of the waves as being gigantic stallions jockeyed by angels, but he had been very young then, only nine.

'So you can manage it yourself?'

'Yes, I think so.'

'I have a bad back. I sprained it a while back.'

Had she sprained it lifting his grandfather?

Staggering with the weight of the suitcase he followed her into the house, into the living-room, which was much smaller than the rooms in his house in Lunderston. He noticed at once the large number of photographs: on the walls, on the chest-of-drawers, on the mantelpiece. He was sure there was none of himself or his mother. It didn't matter. He had brought one with him.

'Is my grandfather asleep?' he asked.

'Yes.'

Perhaps his grandfather had to take pills to make him sleep. Matthew had often stood by his mother's bed watching her sleep and hoping she would not waken because she would then have to suffer pain.

'Did you get something to eat on the plane?' asked his aunt.

'Yes, thank you.' He hadn't, really.

'You'll not be hungry then. Tea's at six.'

She led the way up the stairs. There was no carpet on them. The walls too were bare, with no pictures. It wasn't nearly as comfortable as his own house. He hadn't realised before that this grandfather and his aunt Fiona might be poor.

The room was the one he had shared with his mother. He remembered the magnificent view. His mother and he had looked out at it often.

His nose was runny. Stealthily he wiped it with his hankie. He was reminded of Veronica.

'Have you got a cold?' asked his aunt, as if accusing him.

'I think it was the wind.'

'What are you going to do with yourself till tea-time?'

'I thought I'd go for a walk.'

'Have you brought Wellingtons and a raincoat?'

'Yes.'

'See that you put them on.'

As soon as she was gone he got out of his case the photograph of himself, his mother, and father. It had been taken at the Pencil. His father had his hand on Matthew's shoulder and his mother was laughing.

He put it up on the dressing table. If his aunt ordered him to put it back in his case he would do it, for it was her house, but she couldn't prevent him from taking it out and looking at it.

He looked at it now.

He wished his mother wasn't dead, he wished his father hadn't gone away, he wished there was someone, anyone would do, even Sheila Burnside, to prevent him from wanting to cry.

Sixteen

When he went downstairs Aunt Fiona was in the kitchen, off the living-room. She didn't come out to see him off. When he called that he was going she didn't answer.

Outside the wind almost blew him off his feet. There would be no larks singing in the sky. They would be resting in their nests in the grass. He felt pleased about that. Sheep scampered out of his way, but they didn't go far, they weren't afraid of him. He felt pleased about that too.

In that great expanse of machair he was alone, so that, sorry for himself, he could safely have wept, but he didn't, he couldn't. If he wasn't brave his father would never come home again.

At last, past the dunes with the many rabbit holes, he clambered down on to the sands. They stretched for over a mile. At the far end there were tall smooth rocks forming a labyrinth. He and his mother had played hide-and-seek there.

Where was his mother now? Very near, for he imagined that he could smell her perfume and hear her voice; but also very far away, so far that not even in a space ship that travelled faster than light could he reach her.

He stood and watched gannets plunging into the sea, and seagulls showing off their flying skill in the strong wind. He wished he was a seagull.

As he walked on he picked up some small perfectly shaped shells and put them in his pocket. He would take them home to Mrs Macdonald.

When he reached the tall columns of rock he looked for the one on which he had scratched his name and his mother's: Matthew Sowglass and Catriona McLure. She had wanted him to call her that. It had been Catriona McLure who had played there as a child.

There was no sign now of the names. Rain, wind, and sea had erased them.

Looking at his wristwatch he saw that it was now after five. He mustn't be late for tea, so he walked faster going back.

Suddenly, far ahead, he saw on the high bank a figure, a person, looking down at him. It was a woman, it was Aunt Fiona. Had she come to make sure that he was safe? Or had she hoped that he had been drowned?

As soon as she saw that he had seen her she disappeared. When he got back should he thank her for coming to look for him? Better not.

Tea was a boiled egg, oatcakes, bread and jam. It was eaten in the living-room. The tablecloth was so white he was afraid he would drop yellow yolk on it. Aunt Fiona didn't want to talk, so he kept silent.

His grandfather, he had learned, wasn't in one of the bedrooms upstairs, but was in a bed in the sitting-room downstairs, where it would be easier to attend to him.

There was no television in the house, and no radio. What books he had seen were about religion. It was as well that he had brought some. One was *Kidnapped*. He had read it before. David Balfour's girlfriend was called Catriona.

'If it's all right,' he said, shyly, 'I'll wash the dishes. Mrs Macdonald says I'm quite good at it.'

He got no answer.

He tried again. 'Is your back still sore?'

He wondered if she would be angry if he told her how to take some of the pain out of her back. When he had sprained his ankle Mrs Macdonald had got from the chemist a liniment that had helped. But he couldn't recommend it to Aunt Fiona, for he had forgotten its name and the nearest chemist was in Lochmaddy, ten miles away.

As he washed the dishes in the kitchen, with his sleeves rolled up, he was very careful not to break anything and not to waste the hot water.

Suddenly he was aware that someone was watching him. It was Aunt Fiona. There she was, in the doorway, looking as stern as ever. She had come, he thought, to see if he was making a good job of washing the dishes. But he was wrong. She had a different purpose altogether. She wanted to ask him about his father.

'Where is your father?'

He was immediately on his guard. She was his father's enemy.

'Mrs Macdonald and me think he's in Mexico.'

'Mexico? What's he doing there?'

'Painting. He's a painter, you see. He's a good painter.'

'It's a Catholic country.'

What had that to do with it? He just nodded.

'Why did he go to a Catholic country?'

'I think because there's lots of sunshine. Painters like sunshine. He wouldn't mind if they were Catholics.'

'Because he himself has no religion.'

That wasn't fair to his father. His father had made him wonder about lots of things, more than Mr Henderson the minister had ever done. Wasn't that religious, to wonder about things?

'He just doesn't like to go to church.'

'Doesn't he know that atheists go to hell?'

Matthew smiled. 'He doesn't believe in hell.'

'Then he's got a rude awakening in front of him.'

Somehow – he couldn't have explained why – Matthew found that picture of his father in hell as funny. How could he be sent to a place he didn't believe in?

'He'll never come back. You know that.'

He shook his head. He refused to accept a future that didn't have his father in it.

'How often does he write to you?'

Matthew didn't reply.

'I've been told he never writes.'

Who could have told her that?

Then, to his astonishment, her voice changed, it became hoarse, it pleaded. 'What about me? What's to become of me when he dies? I'll have to leave this house.'

Yes, he supposed the new minister would want to move in.

'Couldn't you go and stay with Aunt Beatrice or Aunt Morag?'

But of course their husbands would object. They didn't like her.

'You're not saying I could go and stay with you.'

He was appalled. 'With me?'

'It's a big house, isn't it? I've got more right than her. I'm kin, she's not.'

'My father said Mrs Macdonald was to look after me.'

'You prefer her to me. Is that what you're saying?'

Yes, that certainly was what he was saying.

Luckily the telephone rang then, in the living-room.

'Maybe it's Mrs Macdonald,' he said. 'She said she would phone every night.'

With her hand on her brow as if she had a headache, Aunt Fiona went to answer it.

'It's for you,' she called.

He tried not to look too eager as he took the telephone.

'It's me, Matthew.'

114

Aunt Fiona went out of the room, still with her hand on her brow.

Mrs Macdonald sounded anxious. 'How are you, son? Did you enjoy the flight?'

'Yes, thank you. I'm fine.'

'What's the weather like?'

'It's very windy. I went for a walk on the sand.'

'By yourself?'

'Yes.'

'Wasn't the sea rough, with the wind?'

'Yes, but I didn't go too near.'

'I should hope not. You'll be very careful, won't you?'

He smiled. She knew he was always careful.

'Sheila phoned. She was quite cross that you'd gone without telling her.'

'I didn't have to tell her.'

'No, but it would have been friendly.' Then she lowered her voice. 'How are they treating you?'

He lowered his voice too. 'All right. I've not seen my grandfather yet. He's always asleep.'

'He'll be sedated.'

'Aunt Fiona's got a sore back.'

'Did she get it humphing peats?' Mrs Macdonald was ashamed of her sarcasm. 'I expect she got it lifting and laying the old man.'

'She wants to come and stay with me when he dies.'

'She what!'

'She'll have to leave the manse, you see.'

'Well, we'll see aboot that, won't we? Is there anybody else there with you?'

'No, there's just me.'

'I'd have thought the place would be hotching with relatives. But I expect they're waiting till he's gone. Lucy's nudging against my legs. I think she kens it's you I'm talking to.'

115

'Give her a pat for me.'

'I'll do that. Take care of yourself now. It's not just Lucy that's missing you.'

He knew she would be in tears as she put the telephone down. She loved him, though she never said so. But then he loved her and he never said so.

Aunt Fiona came in. She did not ask about the telephone call. She said his grandfather was awake and wanted to see him. 'Just for a minute.'

Seventeen

What struck him at once was how small his grandfather looked in the big bed. He seemed to have shrunk and to be still shrinking. He was like a child with a white beard. Not a very nice child really, for he was showing his teeth in a snarl, like Lucy when confronted by a dog, as if he thought everybody was his enemy and he wanted them all to pay for the pain he was suffering. But then Matthew realised it was more likely that it was the pain itself or the fear of the pain that was causing the snarl. Don't be in a hurry to judge, Mrs Macdonald was fond of saying: think of your own faults. Yes, but Matthew could not help remembering that this dying old man had judged without mercy his own daughter, Matthew's mother, and condemned her to hell. Even if hell existed Matthew couldn't see that human beings had any right to say that other human beings should go to it after they died. Surely it should be God who decided that, or the Devil?

He stood by the bed, not knowing what to say, but he had to say something. 'Good evening,' he said. 'I hope you're feeling better.'

His grandfather astonished him, and Aunt Fiona too, by saying, in a hoarse voice, that he wanted to speak 'to the boy' alone.

Aunt Fiona hesitated, was about to say something, and then left in silence.

Matthew felt a little afraid but tried not to show it. He also felt curious. Was his grandfather going to let him into a secret that was to be kept from Aunt Fiona? His grandfather had spent his life in praying, that was to say talking to God, and it could be that God had told him things that few people knew about. Did he want to pass on some of those things to Matthew? After all, Matthew was one of the Elect.

But whatever it was his grandfather wanted to say he never said it. Suddenly his mouth fell open, his eyes bulged, and what he uttered weren't words but meaningless gurgles. Unseen hands seemed to have grabbed him by the throat. His own hands, like claws, gripped the bedclothes and then, as Matthew watched in horrified fascination, slowly let go.

Matthew ran to the door. 'Aunt Fiona,' he called.

When she came she had a dishcloth in her hand. Had she found dishes that he hadn't washed properly?

'What is it?'

'I think grandfather needs his medicine.'

She pushed past him and looked at her father in the bed. She shook her head. 'He's past needing medicine; or anything else.'

It took Matthew a few seconds to grasp what she meant.

'Is he dead?' he whispered.

'Yes, he's dead. What did you say to him?'

'I didn't say anything.'

'What did he say to you?'

'Nothing. He tried to say something but he couldn't.'

Matthew crept over to the bed and gazed down at his grandfather. In that ghastly face – the mouth was still open and the eyes still bulged – he saw a resemblance to his beautiful mother. It was death that was causing the resemblance. All dead people, he vaguely thought, must look alike:

118

those on their way to heaven and those on their way to hell. The living couldn't tell which were which. He remembered what Davy Moore had said about dead people.

Aunt Fiona drew the bedsheet over her father's face.

'Is that what you came for?' she asked.

He didn't understand.

'Who sent you? To see him die. To kill him.'

She didn't know what she was saying. She was too shocked to make sense. Who did she think had sent him?

'Nobody sent me. I just wanted to come.'

'Why did you want to come?'

He could have said, to get away from Sheila Burnside. It would have been true, but there were other reasons that he couldn't have explained.

He noticed that Aunt Fiona wasn't crying. Neither was he. Like him she found it hard to cry. Was it because of their McLure nature, inherited from Grandfather? But when he was alone he cried. He had cried a lot after his mother died and his father went away. He could not imagine his aunt ever crying. Dimly he realised that she should not be blamed but pitied.

'There are things to be done,' she said.

Yes, there was the doctor to be sent for, then the police maybe, and the undertaker. All Grandfather's parishioners would have to be informed, and all his relatives. Soon the manse would be – to use Mrs Macdonald's strange word – hotching with McLures.

Eighteen

They did not all come. Aunt Rachel and Uncle Alan, with their three children, Matthew's cousins, had just arrived in Greece on holiday and decided it would be unreasonable to expect them to hurry, at great inconvenience, to attend a funeral that would last hardly an hour and, to be truthful, would be a pretty dreary affair. That was how Uncle Alan rather peevishly explained it on the telephone, not to Aunt Fiona – he particularly didn't want to speak to *her* – but to Aunt Morag, who said she understood but who, when telling the others, couldn't help being bitter. They had all had to make sacrifices to attend, hadn't they? Rachel had always had that selfish streak. Marrying Alan hadn't improved her.

Aunt Martha mentioned, not for the first time, that her husband, Uncle Robert, had probably jeopardised his promotion prospects by taking time off.

Uncle Robert nodded and sighed.

Matthew, saying nothing, for he wasn't supposed to say anything, sat in the background, watching and listening. Once he overheard his aunts Morag and Martha reminding each other how deprived and unhappy their childhoods had been, because of their father's unfair strictness. So, he reflected, had his mother's childhood been unhappy. She had told him about it.

Once, in the garden, in the corner where the lettuce had grown, he thought of going to Aunt Fiona and telling her that he was sorry but he didn't want to go to the funeral. He wouldn't say it but she would guess that it was because Grandfather hadn't gone to his mother's funeral.

But he got over his huff. The funny thing was, he found that he didn't want to hurt Aunt Fiona's feelings. He still didn't like her and still hadn't forgiven her but he was beginning to respect her. So many things she had believed in she now doubted. She never said it but he could see it in her eyes, and in the way she did things, even little things like setting the table. One big change he noticed. She no longer miscalled his father. It wasn't for his father's sake or for his mother's but for Matthew's. He wondered if she was beginning to like him.

The day of the funeral turned out to be the worst weather for weeks, very wet, with a gale blowing. The graveyard too, with no trees, had only a low drystone dyke for protection. One old woman had her umbrella torn out of her hand. If she hadn't let go she would have gone with it.

The singing of psalms, in Gaelic, had always struck Matthew as weird and mournful. It was particularly so that afternoon, for there was an element of complaint in it. What had they or the dead man done to deserve such weather? Even the sheep were taking shelter. The minister, an old man, had no doubt meant to hold forth for the usual hour or so but he had to be content with thirty-five minutes. Matthew wasn't the only one who kept keeking at his watch.

At the finish they didn't quite rush to the gate and the cars waiting outside but they hurried. There was to be no funeral feasts. That was Uncle Robert's sarcastic description; not even sausage rolls, and certainly no drams. Aunt Fiona was in charge.

In her sodden black coat, and holding on to her hat she stood at the gate thanking them for attending.

When they were all gone she didn't, as her sisters expected, join them in the taxi, but instead walked back into the graveyard, still holding on to her hat. She stood by her father's grave.

It seemed to Matthew unfair that she should be alone, so he crept after her.

One of the gravediggers, a young man in a yellow oilskin coat, gave him a wink. It reassured him but he didn't think he should wink back.

Aunt Fiona turned and gave him a stern look. She still wasn't crying.

'What do you want, Matthew Sowglass?'

He couldn't answer. There were so many things he wanted. The simplest was to get back to the house and change into dry clothes. The hardest was to have his father back.

Nineteen

That evening his aunts and uncles gathered in the big room to discuss what was to be done about Aunt Fiona. She would have to leave the manse soon. The kirk session had offered her the use of a cottage and had promised to do any urgent repairs, but it was very isolated, almost a mile from the public road, reached by a sandy track in very bad repair, and she had no car. Grandfather had left very little money. So the question was, were her sisters, and their husbands, obliged to help her financially. Uncle James did not see that they were. She was a strong able-bodied woman who could surely find work. Anyway, she would be too proud to accept their charity. It wouldn't be charity, said his wife Aunt Morag, indignantly. They owed it to her. In order to look after their father she had given up any chance of marriage and a family of her own.

Matthew sat in a corner, quiet as a mouse and as alert. One of the things he was thinking was that he had thirty-three pounds in his bank account. He was willing to let Aunt Fiona have it all.

Suddenly Uncle Robert caught sight of him and had an idea.

'Why shouldn't she go to Lunderston and look after the boy?'

They all stared at Matthew. They nodded. It seemed a good idea.

'She might not be willing to leave the island,' said Aunt Martha.

'Why not? The rest of you have left. It's a fine big house yonder. She'd be more than comfortable.'

'What if Sowglass came back?' asked Uncle James.

'He's not likely to do that, is he?'

'No, but you never can tell.'

'Wouldn't he be grateful to her for looking after his son?'

It was time for the mouse to squeak. 'I want Mrs Macdonald to look after me. I like her.' He did not say 'love' because nobody in Scotland ever said it, even if they felt it.

Uncle Robert shook his head impatiently. He didn't believe in letting children have their say, especially one who was, to be candid, not all that bright, judging from his long silences. 'Mrs Macdonald's not a relative. Your Aunt Fiona is.'

'Who'll put it to her?' asked Uncle James. 'You, Morag?'

'Martha's older than me.'

'Both of you then. You should be able to make her see that it would be in her best interests, and the boy's too of course.'

Matthew wondered if he should tell them that Aunt Fiona had already, as it were, applied for the job, and he had turned her down.

'I think,' he said, 'Aunt Fiona wants to stay here so that she can look after Grandfather's grave.'

Though it was a shrewd enough remark Uncle Robert saw it as another instance of the boy's simpleness.

'She couldn't do that if she was in Lunderston.'

It wasn't the boy's fault that he was simple, thought Uncle Robert; it was the way he had been brought up.

All the same, he had pointed out a snag. Fiona would want to play the martyr.

'I'd ask her anyway,' muttered Uncle Robert. 'What do you think, Martha?'

What Martha his wife was thinking was that they weren't

being fair to the boy. Her own daughter, Ailie, would be appalled at the thought of having Aunt Fiona to look after her.

'What do you say, Matthew? Would you like Aunt Fiona to look after you?'

'I want Mrs Macdonald to look after me.' He put on what Mrs Macdonald called his determined face. 'My father said she should.'

'I don't suppose', muttered Uncle Robert, 'they could both look after him?'

The others shook their heads. Aunt Fiona and Mrs Macdonald hated each other.

'So I'm afraid it'll have to be the cottage,' said Uncle James.

'But, James,' said his wife, 'it's so unsuitable. It's at the back of beyond.'

A Glasgow man, Uncle James thought that all Uist was at the back of beyond.

Aunt Fiona then came in and they began to talk about the arrangements for their flight home tomorrow.

Twenty

Next day the sun shone, so Aunt Fiona and Matthew went to the airport to see them off. In private Aunt Morag had asked him if he wanted to go with them and had been surprised when he had replied that he would like to stay for a few days more. She could hardly believe it. After all he had more reason than any of them to resent Fiona because of the way she had treated his mother, and the many bitter things she had said about his father. It looked as if Robert might be right. The boy was a bit simple. That was why he found it easy to forgive.

With tears in her eyes, Aunt Morag embraced him. He was, in appearance, so like Catriona, his mother.

He couldn't have told her why he wanted to stay on. He didn't know himself.

It wasn't because he was afraid of Sheila Burnside. In fact, he had made up his mind that he was going to tell her that if she didn't stop trying to frighten him with her stupid lies he wouldn't want to see her again.

He felt, vaguely, that here in the Hebrides where his mother had been born he was closer to her than beside her grave in Lunderston cemetery. Also he felt that here where it was so beautiful and peaceful he would be able to store up the patience and hope that he would need as he waited for his father to come back.

His aunts gave him kisses and his uncles, just as surreptitiously, money, just before they went out to board the plane. They all told him to be sure and keep in touch when he returned to Lunderston.

Their leave-taking of Aunt Fiona was awkward. Even her sisters weren't sure whether to kiss her or just shake her hand. They didn't know what to say.

One curt nod was all she gave them. They had to share it among them.

It was, as Aunt Morag was to say, bitterly, on the plane, a typical McLure farewell.

In the taxi Aunt Fiona asked the driver to put them down not at the manse but at the road-end leading to the cottage that would soon be her new home.

Dugald offered to drive them right up to the cottage, in spite of the condition of the track, but she said no, it was a fine morning for a walk. He was doubtful. He knew Miss McLure was a great walker, but what about the boy? They would have covered six miles by the time they got back to the manse.

Shyly Matthew said he would like to walk.

There was a breeze but it was light and full of fragrance from the many wild flowers. The machair shone like the sky, only it was green while the sky was blue. Larks sang all the time and curlews called now and then. The sea could be heard, not stormy like yesterday, but gentle, as if its anger was past.

'Am I walking too fast for you?' asked his aunt.

She was, a bit, but he didn't like to say so.

She walked a little slower.

He would have liked to ask if her back was sore but she might think he was sooking up to her.

He was wearing the black tie that had been given him for

the funeral, but in her tweed costume he could make out almost every colour but black. No one could have told she was in mourning. Her head was bare and the sun made her hair look more white than grey. He knew she was not nearly as old as Mrs Macdonald.

He knew why Aunt Morag had been so surprised when he had said he wanted to stay on. They thought Aunt Fiona was his enemy. They knew how cruel she had been to his mother, and that she hated his father. They had heard her say spiteful, untrue things about Mrs Macdonald. So she was his enemy and he should have hated her.

But he didn't hate her. He had tried but he couldn't. He knew that she was unhappy but was too proud to show it: just like him. She prayed. He had seen her on her knees. But what did she say in her prayers, what did she ask for? Perhaps she was too proud to ask for anything.

'You're very quiet,' she said.

'I'm sorry. I was thinking.'

She seemed to smile. 'You're a great one for thinking, Matthew Sowglass. What were you thinking?'

He could hardly tell her the truth and he didn't want to lie. So he said nothing and took care not to step on a cowpat.

'But I've got no right to ask, have I?'

Again he said nothing.

'I was thinking too.'

But she did not say what she was thinking.

In front of them, though still a long way off, was the cottage. There was no other house in sight. Her neighbours would be cattle, sheep, rabbits, and maybe seals, for the sea was close enough for them to slither up. In a storm the cottage would be drenched with spray.

He felt sorry for her at having to live in so lonely a place. It was beautiful and peaceful now, in the sunshine, but at night, in the winter, it would be frightening. It would be so dark you wouldn't be able to see your hand if you held it before your eyes. There was no light from distant street lamps. There was no electricity in the house, only oil lamps that cast eerie shadows.

'It's quite big,' he said.

'Plenty of room for you to come here on your holidays.'

'I would like that.'

'Would you? Would you really?'

'Yes, I would.'

'Perhaps there's someone you would like to bring with you, a friend.'

He would have liked to bring Davy Moore. Davy would have loved this place, but only for a little while. He preferred shops and streets and people.

'I'm sure you have lots of friends.'

'Not an awful lot.'

The truth was, he had none.

He was well known in Lunderston, as a Sowglass who owned the Gallery; as a boy whose mother had died and whose father had gone off and left him. At school his classmates respected him because he was clever, wore good clothes, and wasn't conceited. He liked nearly everybody, but that didn't mean they were his friends. Not even Davy Moore had been his friend. He always kept out of things. He didn't want to but somehow he did. Sheila Burnside thought she was his friend.

'Is this you thinking again?' asked his aunt. She seemed amused.

They were now close to the cottage. It had no garden, the whole machair was its garden. There was no wall or fence: sheep and cattle could come right up to the front door. Everywhere were sheep's pellets and cow-pats. The door was painted blue. There was a pile of peats covered by a tarpaulin.

The door wasn't locked. In Lunderston if you didn't lock your door vandals would go in and do damage. Not only in Lunderston. Mrs Macdonald was always saying that nowhere in the world was safe. She was wrong. Here you would be safe, except maybe from ghosts. Did he believe in ghosts? Not when the sun was shining like now, but when dark came it would be different.

They went in. The rooms were empty but very clean. Grandfather's parishioners had been busy making it ready. From every window there was a splendid view.

How, though, was Aunt Fiona to do her shopping? She had a bicycle but you couldn't carry much on a bicycle, and the nearest shop was five miles away. A van would call once a week, bringing all kinds of things, like potatoes and vegetables. Matthew felt relieved. She was his enemy but he didn't like to think of her in difficulties.

He asked who had lived there.

'An old lady, Mrs McDougall. Everybody called her Shona.'

'Was she very old?'

'She was eighty-two when she died.'

'Did she live here alone?'

'She did. We often visited her.'

'Did my mother visit her?'

It was a terrible thing to ask, but he wasn't sorry he'd asked it.

He waited for the sharp, angry answer.

'I think, of us all, she liked your mother best.'

He saw what an effort it had been for her to say that, not because it was a lie but because it was the truth. His mother when a child had been very happy, in spite of her father's strictness. In every photograph she was laughing. There was one on the dressing table in Matthew's room in Lunderston.

He could easily imagine that smiling black-haired girl gathering flowers on the machair and bringing them to this cottage to give to the old woman. She had loved flowers and yet, like her father who had hated them, she hadn't wanted any at her funeral.

'Most people did,' said his aunt.

Leaving the house, Aunt Fiona closed the front door carefully, to make sure that sheep didn't butt their way in, but she didn't lock it. She couldn't, for there was no key. It must have got lost. It worried Matthew a little. It wasn't likely that in this lonely peaceful place someone wicked would come and harm Aunt Fiona, but you never knew. Nobody had ever thought there would be a murderer in Lunderston.

They walked on in silence for a while.

'What do you want to be when you grow up?' his aunt asked.

'I don't know. Mrs Macdonald thinks I should be a doctor.'

'Why does she think that?'

'She says I listen carefully to what people say to me.'

'So you do.'

'But I don't think I could be a doctor.'

'Why not, if you're so suitable?'

He could never be a doctor because he did not like people to touch him. Mrs Macdonald had noticed; it had amused her. The only exception had been his mother. Once, when Sheila Burnside had tried to grab his hand he had pulled it back, as if, she'd said, scornfully, hers was red-hot.

Perhaps it was because he was one of the Elect. He was always forgetting that.

'I think I would like to be a painter,' he said, boldly. 'But I'm not good enough. When he was my age my father won prizes for drawing and painting.'

He looked about him. It was when his father had come to the Hebrides to paint that he had met Matthew's mother. For that reason, and another, the place was sacred to him. Here he had discovered that he was one of the Chosen.

Twenty-One

M rs Macdonald usually telephoned in the evening, after six, when it was cheaper, but two days before Matthew was to return home her call came before nine in the morning, while he was having his breakfast.

Aunt Fiona, thinking it must be for her, got up to answer it.

He was trying to make up his mind whether or not he liked porridge the way she made it, as thick as mud, when she said, 'It's for you.'

It could only be Mrs Macdonald, but why was she calling him so early? His heart leapt. Had a letter come from his father?

'Is it Mrs Macdonald?'

'Yes. It's a very bad line.'

He got up and took the telephone. His hands were shaking.

To his surprise his aunt laid her hand on his head, as lightly as a fly and as quick to come off again. Then she went into the kitchen, to let his conversation with Mrs Macdonald be private.

'Hello. It's me, Matthew. Is there anything wrong?'

'Yes, son, there's something wrong, terribly wrong.'

A letter had come, but it had not said his father was coming home, it had said his father was dead.

It was certainly a bad line. The sea seemed to be surging over the wires.

'It's Sheila Burnside's father. He's dead. Drowned.'

He stopped breathing. 'Drowned?'

'A yacht race. Yesterday. A fun thing, it was supposed to be. They have it every year. Father and son or daughter. Sheila was crewing for her father. It seems the wind got up suddenly. They were going round Buttock Point on the island.'

Usually the name caused a smile, but not now.

'Mr Burnside fell overboard. He must have lost his balance. Poor Sheila wasn't able to save him. She got hurt herself. They're saying she's a heroine.'

They could be saying she was a murderess. But he was the only one who knew that and he could never say it to anyone.

'Wasn't he wearing a life-jacket?'

'Yes, but it didn't do him much good, did it?'

'Why did he fall overboard. He's used to sailing.'

'Accidents happen.'

'Was it an accident?'

'Good heavens, Matthew, what else could it have been?'

'Yes.'

'Poor lassie. First her mother and now her father. She insisted on going out in the launch looking for him.'

'Did they find him?'

'No, they didn't. I think they've given up hope of finding him alive. An aunt has come from Glasgow to look after Sheila. I'm sorry, Matthew, to have to give you this awful news, but I thought you'd like to know. I expect Sheila will give you a call herself.'

'Why should she give me a call?'

'She's your friend, isn't she?'

He shook his head but of course she couldn't see him.

'I'll be in Glasgow airport on Wednesday to meet you. Give my regards to your aunt.'

134

'Yes, I will.'

He put down the telephone.

His aunt came in. She noticed how pale he was, how he seemed to have difficulty in breathing. 'Bad news?' she asked.

'Yes.'

When he went back to Lunderston he would have to face Sheila. Even if he stayed here he wouldn't be able to escape from her. She would telephone every day. She might even come. Nowhere would he be safe from her.

'Not about your father, I hope.'

'No. Sheila's father.'

'Who is Sheila?'

'A girl I know.'

'What's happened to her father?'

'He's been drowned.'

'How did it happen?'

'It was in a yacht race. An accident. Sheila was with him.'

'Is she all right?'

'Yes.'

'When was this?'

'On Sunday. They often have yacht races on Sundays.'

She didn't say, but he knew she was thinking it, that people who broke the Sabbath shouldn't be surprised if they were punished. But why weren't the others who had taken part in the race punished too? Why had God chosen to punish Mr Burnside? Or was it Sheila who was being punished? That made sense, if, that was, she really had pushed her father overboard. But no, it didn't make sense, for it meant that she had been allowed to do the evil thing that she had planned to do . . . God hadn't punished her. He had helped her.

'Mrs Macdonald sends her regards.'

'That was kind of her. What did he do, Mr Burnside?'

'He was the Sheriff Clerk. He went to church every Sunday.'

'It is what's in your heart that counts. God is not mocked.'
She began to gather the dishes off the table.

It seemed to him God was easily deceived. Meanwhile he
would wait, with dread, for Sheila to call.

Twenty-Two

H e spent Tuesday on the seashore watching birds and then cycling to Lochmaddy to buy presents for Mrs Macdonald and his aunt.

It was easy to choose one for Mrs Macdonald: a small plate decorated with Uist scenes and inscribed 'A present from Uist', to add to her collection of such plates. She often said, 'One day there will be one from Mexico, you'll see.'

He could think of nothing suitable for Aunt Fiona, so she bought a box of ladies' hankies, white with tartan borders, though he had never seen her wipe her nose, or her eyes either.

They were at tea when the call came.

'It's for you,' said his aunt. 'Sheila.'

He felt afraid and resentful. 'I don't want to speak to her. Tell her I'm not here.'

'That would be a lie, Matthew. It would also be unkind. The poor girl will be suffering great grief.'

When he had been suffering great grief his aunt hadn't been kind to him.

He got up and took the telephone.

His aunt quietly left the room.

'It's me, Matthew.'

He had expected her to sound eager and pleased with

herself, but no, she sounded subdued, as if she had been weeping and might weep again soon. It was as if she thought she was talking to someone else, and not to him.

But what she said was for him alone.

'I told you I'd do it. Well, I've done it.'

He didn't know what to say.

'You know what I'm talking about. Mrs Macdonald said she'd told you.'

'She said it was an accident.'

'That's what they all think. That's what I want them to think. We know it wasn't an accident. Just you and me.'

'I don't know it. It could be one of your lies.'

'It's the truth, and you helped me to do it.'

'How did I help you?'

'You knew I was going to do it. You didn't tell anyone, did you? You let me do it, so you're what they call my accomplice.'

'But if you did it I didn't want you to do it.'

'Why didn't you tell Mrs Macdonald?'

'She wouldn't have believed me.'

'That's right. Nobody would have believed you. When are you coming home?'

'Tomorrow.'

'I'll see you then.'

No, you won't, he said, but he said it to himself.

She was mad and only he knew it.

Aunt Fiona came back and sat at the table.

'Finish your tea', she said, sensibly.

The only thing to do, now and afterwards, was to act as if everything was normal.

'I hope you were kind to her.'

She's got some cheek, Mrs Macdonald would have said. When was *she* kind to anyone?

People would be kind to him. But the terrible secret he

shared with Sheila would make their kindness harder to bear than cruelty.

The only sounds then were the ticking of the clock on the mantelpiece, his crunching of the bannocks, some oyster-catchers piping outside, and his aunt sighing.

Why was she sighing? She didn't know about him and Sheila. If she had known what would she have done?

He couldn't think of confiding in her, or in anyone, not even his father if he came home. He would have to suffer alone, not just now but all his life.

He found himself sighing too.

'One day, Matthew, you must bring her here for a holiday.'

He let it pass. It would never happen. It mustn't. This was the very place Sheila might choose to destroy him.

Twenty-Three

He had been wondering if she would kiss him, on the cheek, as some women did, but he didn't think she would. If she did he wouldn't shrink back or in any way show he was embarrassed, though he would be, a bit. Perhaps she would just pat him on the head, as she had already done, more than once. That was her side of it. What about his own? Should he offer to kiss her, on the cheek? But he never kissed Mrs Macdonald. Should he hug her? No. Perhaps he should just offer to shake hands, as adults did. It would look silly, him so wee and her so tall, but nobody would be looking.

'Thank you very much, Aunt Fiona,' he said, gravely, as he was about to join the other passengers boarding the plane. 'I have enjoyed myself very much.'

'Come again then.'

What had Mrs Macdonald said? That she barked like a seal. So she did, but yesterday he had heard real seals barking and they hadn't sounded unfriendly.

'And bring your friend Sheila.'

That shocked him but he managed to smile.

He held out his hand.

Suddenly she crouched and embraced him. In his confusion he couldn't be sure that he had seen tears in her eyes.

Then he hurried towards the plane. He had let his mother,

and his father, down, by being friendly with their enemy. For surely Aunt Fiona had been his mother's enemy and still was his father's. He should hate her, and he did hate her, as much as he could hate anyone, which wasn't much. But he understood her better now and he had discovered that all her life she had felt lonely, in spite of having so many sisters.

The stewardess welcomed him aboard. 'Hello, young traveller. Did you have a good time?'

'Yes, thank you.'

'You've been out in the sun. I can see that.'

Looking out of the window, he saw, far below, the cottage his aunt would be living in, at the edge of the sea. There were sheep but they didn't bother to stop grazing, they were used to this great noisy bird flying over them.

Soon his aunt would be living there alone. Would she ever come to the door and wave? He did not think so. It would be a long time before she was ready to do that.

He thought of his father and for a few seconds did what he had always resolutely refused to do. He reproached him for staying away so long and for not writing.

Twenty-Four

At Glasgow airport, outside the barrier where people were gathered to greet their friends, he caught sight of Mrs Macdonald waving wildly. Beside her, not waving at all, was Sheila Burnside, with her hair tied by a black ribbon: her only sign of mourning.

He felt alarmed. Among all those smiling happy faces hers was the only one with evil intent. One look was all he needed. Everyone else saw her as a young girl in mourning for someone she had loved. They gazed at her with sympathy and admiration. He saw her as an agent of the Devil. If he shouted it out they would think he was mad, and maybe he was, infected by her.

Mrs Macdonald embraced him. 'You're looking well. Isn't he, Sheila?'

Sheila studied him. 'Isn't he a bit pale? But then he's always pale.'

'No, he isn't. I think he's nicely sunburnt.'

Sheila insisted on carrying his suitcase. She had boasted that she was stronger than he and had proved it several times.

As they made for the exit, through the press of people, he and Mrs Macdonald were momentarily separated from Sheila.

'Why did you bring her?' he asked.

Mrs Macdonald was surprised not just by the question but also by the quiet passion with which it was spoken.

'She wanted to come. I thought it was nice of her. She's had a terrible shock, remember. She's staying with us.'

Before he could ask what she meant Sheila rejoined them.

Nothing more was said until they were in the car on their way to Lunderston. Sheila sat in the back.

Suddenly she touched him on the shoulder. 'They've found the body. On the island, wedged among rocks.'

She said it as if it was an ordinary thing.

'You wouldn't have known it was him, his face was so smashed.'

'Please, Sheila,' said Mrs Macdonald.

Trying to be fair, he remembered how he himself had spoken and what he had spoken about, after his mother had died. Everybody had said how brave he was for not crying. At Davy Moore's funeral he hadn't cried either, though everybody else had, except Davy's mother. Could it be that Sheila and he did have the same kind of nature?

'Sheila got hurt,' said Mrs Macdonald. 'She's a mass of black and blue bruises. It's a wonder she can walk. She should be in bed.'

'You should see my backside,' said Sheila. 'It's like a huge grape.'

'Sheila, please!' said Mrs Macdonald.

'I'm staying with you,' said Sheila.

'Why?'

'Because I want to and Mrs Macdonald says I can. We knew you wouldn't mind. Do you mind?'

'Of course he doesn't,' said Mrs Macdonald.

'I thought you'd want to go back to Glasgow.'

Where, she'd said, she had killed the baby in the pram.

'I hate Glasgow. I want to stay in Lunderston.'

'Will your people let you?'

'It's got nothing to do with them.'

'I'm afraid it has, Sheila,' said Mrs Macdonald. 'But we'll see. In the meantime we've got plenty of room and you and Matthew will be company for each other.'

'The funeral's on Saturday,' said Sheila, in that casual voice. 'In Glasgow. It's not really a funeral. He's going to be burned, not buried.'

'Are you going?'

'I'm thinking about it.'

'Don't talk like that, Sheila,' said Mrs Macdonald. 'I know how upset you are but people who don't know you wouldn't understand.'

If she lives with us, thought Matthew, Mrs Macdonald will surely find out her true nature.

Someone must find that out soon, if he was to be saved from her.

Lucy met them in the hall, mewing, with her tail up.

'She's glad you're back, Matthew,' cried Mrs Macdonald.

'Cats don't have affections,' said Sheila. 'That's why I like them.'

Too late she remembered that she and Matthew weren't alone.

Mrs Macdonald still made allowances. Small wonder poor Sheila felt distrust, even of cats. 'I'm sure Lucy's fond of Matthew. She's known him all her life.'

When Mrs Macdonald stooped to stroke Lucy the cat drew back.

'That's what I mean. You're the one that feeds her, Mrs Macdonald. So why isn't she fond of you?'

'She is, in her own way. She often sits on my lap.'

'When it suits her. Cats only do what suits them.'

'People do, Sheila, most of the time.'

Mrs Macdonald spoke sharply. Matthew wondered if she was already having second thoughts about Sheila.

Sheila had asked for and been given his mother's room. 'Just temporarily,' Mrs Macdonald whispered to him. 'How could I have said no?'

Once, when he and Sheila were alone in the room she said: 'Do you know why I like it? It smells of death.'

He remembered those awful weeks when his mother lay dying, often in pain, dosed with drugs.

'My mother didn't die here. She died in hospital.'

That conversation took place after the cremation of Mr Burnside and before the meeting with Sheila's relatives, which was to decide where she was to stay, either in Glasgow with one of them or in Lunderston with Matthew and Mrs Macdonald.

They all tried to humour her. She was distressed by her father's sudden death, or so they thought. Her father, a thrifty man, had left her quite a lot of money and the bungalow was worth at least thirty thousand pounds. She would have to wait till she was twenty-one but that she would possess it one day gave her authority now.

If her relatives had come thinking that in her grief she would be easily persuaded they quickly found how wrong they were.

They were curiously uneasy when speaking to her. Matthew was to discover the reason when he overheard her two aunts whispering to each other. He gathered that Sheila, when eight, had needed psychiatric treatment.

'I can pay for my board and lodging,' she said.

'That's not the point, Sheila,' said her uncle, her father's brother. 'You're a minor. You're too young to decide these things for yourself.'

'And really, Sheila,' said her aunt, her mother's sister, 'you should be staying with your own family.'

'Do you want me to stay with you, Aunt Sarah?

145

That direct question flustered Aunt Sarah. 'Of course, my dear, if that's what you want.'

'Well, thanks very much, but it's not what I want. I want to stay here with Matthew and Mrs Macdonald.'

Matthew sat by the window, silent and unheeded.

'If they say I can then it's settled.'

'I'm afraid it's not as simple as that, Sheila,' said her uncle. 'There are legal requirements.'

'Mrs Macdonald, tell them I can stay here.'

Mrs Macdonald was embarrassed. 'Matthew and I would be pleased to have you, Sheila, but your relatives would have to agree.'

'It's none of their business.'

'It is our business,' said her aunt. 'I'm sure your mother would have wanted you to come and stay with us in Glasgow, and go to Hutcheson Grammar, which was her school.' She sobbed.

'Lunderston High suits me.'

Matthew could tell that in spite of what they said they weren't all that keen to have her. They knew things about her that made them wary.

'Shouldn't you have Matthew's father's permission?' asked her aunt. 'It's his house.'

'No, it isn't. It's Matthew's. Anyway, how can I get his permission when he's dead?'

'Dead? I didn't know he was dead.'

'Nobody knows that,' said Mrs Macdonald, sharply. 'Sheila, you had no right to say that.'

'Well, he hasn't written for years.'

'That doesn't mean he's dead. We have reason to believe he's alive.'

Mr Baird, the lawyer, still sent money every month. But, as he had pointed out, someone else could be pocketing it in that far-off place in Mexico.

'He's not dead,' muttered Matthew, but nobody heard or heeded him.

'What if he came back?' asked Aunt Sarah.

'What difference would it make?' said Sheila.

'If Mr Sowglass came back,' said Mrs Macdonald, 'and he will some day, I'm sure of that, he would have no objection to Sheila being here. He's an easy-going kind of man.'

'Too easy-going, if you ask me,' said the other aunt, who did not approve of fathers, even if they were artists, deserting their children.

Sheila went over to Matthew. 'What do you think?' she asked. 'Do *you* want me to stay with you?'

She was challenging him. He should have said boldly that he didn't want her. She would have too many opportunities to make him as evil as herself. But he lacked the courage.

'I want what Mrs Macdonald wants.'

It was what a confused, timid, not very bright, dependent boy would have said, and that was what they all, even Mrs Macdonald, thought he was.

'It's what Sheila wants that counts,' said Mrs Macdonald. 'She's the one that's suffering.'

So it was settled. Sheila would stay in Lunderston for a trial period of unspecified length.

Her uncles and aunts pretended to be disappointed but it seemed to Matthew that they were greatly relieved.

Twenty-Five

W hen her relatives were gone, Sheila came knocking on the door of his room. It was the first time he had ever locked it. He had felt that from the beginning he must protect himself from her.

She knocked harder. 'It's me, Sheila.'

He went over to the door. He had been writing a letter to Aunt Fiona. Usually he did his writing, and reading, in the kitchen, but that sanctuary was no longer safe.

'What do you want?' he asked. 'I'm busy.'

'Why have you locked the door?'

He imagined her sneering at his foolishness. Did a spider sneer when it saw a fly approaching.

'I want to tell you something.'

'What is it?'

'Let me in and I'll tell you.'

He did not have to be afraid of her. As one of the Chosen he was under God's special protection. Whatever happened no harm could come to him. He still believed that, though not so wholeheartedly as he had done years ago when he had pee'd on his grandfather's lettuce. He did not trust God so much now.

He opened the door.

She came in, limping a little. She had been hurt in the accident. If she was in pain she would never show it.

'What were you busy doing?'

'Writing a letter.'

'To your father?'

He wrote letters to his father but never sent them.

'To my Aunt Fiona.'

She gave Pegasus a pat on the haunch as she went over to the window. Sunset turned the Firth red.

'What a splendid view you have.'

Were wicked people able to enjoy beautiful things? Mr Henderson didn't seem to think so, but Matthew's father had once told him that in Italy hundreds of years ago cruel princes had paid artists to paint beautiful pictures.

'I want to tell you something,' she said.

He should have said he didn't want to hear it.

'You know things about me that nobody else does.'

'I know you tell stupid lies.'

'How do you know they're lies?'

Because, he thought, nobody as young as you could be as wicked as you claim to be.

But was that true? Mrs Macdonald often looked up from her newspaper and said what little monsters children could be.

'Have they found the person who killed Davy Moore?' she asked.

Several suspects had been arrested but had been let go.

He could imagine her prowling in the dark, but could he imagine her striking Davy on the head with the half brick? Yes, he could.

'Do you know why I did it? He disgusted me. Little creeps like him disgust me. They should all be exterminated.'

'Did the baby in the pram disgust you?'

'All babies are disgusting.'

'Your father, did he disgust you?'

'Him especially. I told you why.'

'Does everybody disgust you?'

'Everybody but you, Matthew.' She laughed.

'What was it you wanted to tell me?'

'Oh yes. I wanted to promise that I would do nothing while I'm staying in your house. I mean, I won't kill anyone.' She laughed again. 'Unless you want me to.'

Did she really think that he would want her to kill someone on his behalf?

Twenty-Six

In a small compact town like Lunderston, where everybody discussed everybody else's business, more often with good nature than malice, it soon became generally known that Bella Macdonald, guardian of the boy Matthew Sowglass, had agreed to take in the poor lassie Sheila Burnside, whose father had so tragically been drowned. It was taken for granted that Bella wasn't doing it solely out of the goodness of her heart. The girl had been left well provided for and could pay her way, but it was still an act of Christian kindness, not to say of courage, for Sheila would need not just looking after in the physical sense, but very careful comforting too. The boy was a sad wee soul with a dead mother and a father God knew where, and Bella had a difficult enough job with him and was coping with it very well. To her embarrassment she was praised in kirk, from the pulpit. Every head turned to smile at her where she sat at the back with her two young charges, who looked, the girl especially, decorously dressed and properly humble. They were, and would be in the future, a credit to the church, the town, Bella, and themselves. There was quite a display of dabbing at eyes with Sunday-best hankies.

At school, where they were both in the top class of the First Year, 1A, which included Latin in the subjects it studied, their teachers were delighted and their classmates interested and on the whole well disposed, though inevitably with a few cases of envy. Everything was easy for this brilliant pair. In the staff-room it was confidently predicted that one day they would be girl-dux and boy-dux respectively, with their names in gold on the board of honour. They would then go on to univerity, either Glasgow or Edinburgh, where they would achieve honours degrees. As likely as not they would continue their studies at Oxford or Cambridge. They deserved it all, to compensate for their previous ill luck.

It was noticed too how, in spite of their outstanding talents, they remained modest and helpful, especially the girl. Unlike him she was also good at sports. Though only a first-year pupil she was soon a member of the second-eleven hockey team, among girls two or three years older, and in the gymnastics class she excelled at activities that required nerve as well as agility, such as vaulting over the wooden horse and clambering up ropes. She was also a strong bold swimmer, as indeed had been demonstrated when she had striven so bravely but alas in vain to save her father. Above all she was so good-looking, with her long blonde hair, fair skin, delicate mouth, and frank blue eyes. Already she showed signs of having an enviable figure.

There were of course a few detractors. Some of those who had been in Miss Johnston's class in the primary school remembered how she had clyped on wee Davy Moore. But these, being dunces, were now in low classes like 1E and 1F and did not come into contact with her. One or two of the stupidest and most prurient, in the lavatory where they were stealing sly puffs, muttered that she and Sowglass groped each other in the big swanky house on the sea-front; but not even those who made the foul accusation really believed it. She was too superior and wholesome, he too lacking in enterprise.

As for Mrs Macdonald, she began to see them as brother and sister; and, when she had allowed herself an extra sherry, imagined that they were her own children. She had never been happier in her life. What pleased her most was that the strange animosity that Matthew had once shown towards Sheila seemed to have vanished. He was as proud of her achievements as a brother. As well as a good player of the piano she had a fine singing voice. At a concert where she sang in aid of funds for the local Oxfam shop Matthew, Mrs Macdonald noted, clapped as loudly as any. It was Sheila who was chosen to present the cheque. 'You're doing a fine job with that lassie, Bella,' Mrs Oliphant said, and added, not quite so enthusiastically, 'and with the boy too.'

Sometimes Mrs Macdonald let herself dream that Sheila was really Anabel, though she was tall for her age and fair-haired whereas Anabel would have been dumpy and dark, like Mrs Macdonald herself. Besides, Anabel would have been a woman of thirty-five.

At Christmas both Sheila and Matthew were members of the school choir that went round old folks' homes singing carols.

Then, six weeks before Easter, it all changed.

Twenty-Seven

It was a Thursday morning. Mrs Macdonald was in the house alone when the postman brought the mail, two bills, some circulars and a postcard. She looked at the picture. It showed, in bright colours, a long wide avenue, with trees and statues. She looked closer. It was a view of Mexico City. She turned it over. The stamp was Mexican. The handwriting, what little there was of it, just one line, was familiar: it was Mr Sowglass's. So was the signature or rather the two scribbled initials H.S. 'Returning home soon.' That was all. No mention of his son. It was addressed to her.

With all the strength drained from her hands she could hardly hold the card. How soon was soon? Could it be today, tomorrow, or next month? She didn't know whether to be overjoyed for Matthew's sake or alarmed for her own. It had long been her fear that Sowglass would come home and marry again, some young woman who wouldn't want or need a housekeeper.

Thinking, wildly, that it could be a forgery or hoax or mistake of some kind, she telephoned Mr Baird the lawyer and was told by his secretary that he too that morning had received a similar vague message.

In her desperation she thought of withholding the news from Matthew, for a little while anyway. Mr Sowglass had

154

shown that he wasn't reliable, to say the least, so it was quite possible that he would take his time about returning home. Mexico City, as she found from the atlas, was on his route home but he might decide to linger there for a while or to visit other cities in Mexico and America. He might be away for several weeks or months longer.

These were unworthy, disloyal thoughts. She was ashamed of them. She would show the postcard to Matthew the minute he stepped inside the door. Strictly speaking, it wasn't his but hers, since it was addressed to her.

Looking out of the window, she saw that it had begun to snow. Why had Sowglass chosen to leave a warm country like Mexico to face a Scottish winter?

When Matthew and Sheila came home from school they were already excited, because of the snow. Sheila talked about sledging.

Mrs Macdonald watched them taking off their raincoats, dark blue in Matthew's case, red in Sheila's. The contrast, she thought, summed up the difference in their natures, he so reserved and withdrawn, she so outgoing, so ready for everything.

'Look what I've got,' she said, taking the postcard from her apron pocket.

She had meant to say it joyfully and triumphantly but it came out hoarse and shaky. She was on the verge of weeping.

Sheila snatched the postcard. One glance, and she knew what it meant. A look of mingled fury and jealousy flashed across her face. It lasted only a few moments but Mrs Macdonald would remember it with horror all her life.

Afraid that Sheila might tear it up Mrs Macdonald took the postcard and handed it to Matthew. 'From your father. He says he's coming home. It's really addressed to me, but it's meant for you.'

Matthew looked at the card and then rushed upstairs with it to his room, like Lucy with a mouse she was afraid would be taken from her.

Sheila and Mrs Macdonald stared at each other.

'I was sure he was dead,' said Sheila, meaning that she had hoped it.

Mrs Macdonald did not have the hypocrisy to rebuke her. Hadn't she cherished the same hope now and then?

'What's going to happen to me?' asked Sheila. 'You'll be all right. Matthew won't let him send you away. But he'll be glad to get rid of me.'

'He'll have to do what his father tells him. We should be glad for his sake, Sheila. He's waited a long time for this.'

'If I was him I wouldn't get too excited.'

'What do you mean?'

'It's sure to be a great let-down.'

'Why?'

'Because it always is.'

Twenty-Eight

As he read over and over again the three magical words 'Returning home soon' in his mind was the memory of the small beetle which he had killed but which had come alive again. His relief had made the sky more radiant. Everything had come right again.

Now another miracle was about to take place. It couldn't make everything right, for his mother had died and nothing could ever make that right, but when his father came home he would feel happier and safer than he had done since his mother's death.

Lucy had come upstairs after him and was sitting on his bed washing her face. She paused, to stare at him and mew, as if she was happy because he was.

He gazed at the photograph of his mother and father on the dressing table. It had been taken just after they were married. Both were smiling, but it had always seemed to him that his mother's smile was a little uncertain, as if she was afraid that her happiness would not last and would have to be paid for.

His grandfather's curse had been upon her then. It had worried her, for though she had said that she did not believe in curses she could not help being affected. Unlike his father she had believed in God.

With His usual patience God had waited till Matthew was ten before striking her with the cancer that had caused her great pain and then had killed her.

The bearded man beside her, her husband and Matthew's father, had cried bitterly – Matthew had heard him – that God had nothing to do with it, it was just bad luck.

Perhaps in Mexico, which Mrs Macdonald had said was a religious country his father had come to believe in God.

But did it matter whether you called it bad luck or God's anger?

With the postcard in his pocket he went downstairs to the kitchen where Mrs Macdonald was preparing the tea and Sheila was reading the day's newspaper.

He wanted to share his happiness with them, but it wouldn't be easy in Sheila's case. She hadn't wanted his father to come home.

She looked up. 'Well, have you had a good wee greet?' she asked, contemptuously.

Greet was a Scots word meaning weep.

'Why should he greet?' cried Mrs Macdonald. 'With such good news?'

'Mrs Macdonald and I think you shouldn't build your hopes up too high.'

Mrs Macdonald was indignant. 'I said nothing of the kind. I said your father might be delayed, that's all.'

'It says soon.'

'Aye, but he might want to visit other places on his way home.'

'But that would mean he'd be just a little late.'

'That's a' it would mean.' Suddenly Mrs Macdonald burst out crying and hid her face in her apron. 'I'm crying, son, but I'm happy for you. You've waited so long.'

He felt the threat of tears in his own eyes. It was because he loved her.

Sheila's eyes were dry. 'He'll have to come by plane. Planes crash.'

Mrs Macdonald's face appeared, shocked and tearful. 'What a thing to say! Sheila, you should be ashamed of yourself. Are you trying to ruin Matthew's happiness?'

'I'm trying to warn him. He thinks everything's going to be all right. But it's never all right. How long has his father been away? Three years. He couldn't have been a very loving father, could he?'

'He went away because my mother died.'

'That was why,' said Mrs Macdonald. But she didn't altogether believe it. There had to be another reason. Not all men fled to the far ends of the earth when their wives died.

'He went away because he wanted to become a better painter,' said Sheila.

That, thought Mrs Macdonald, could have some truth in it. Was it spite that had given Sheila such insight?

'He's coming home to sell his paintings,' said Sheila. 'He won't stay in Lunderston. It'll be too dull for him. He'll go away again.'

She went out. They heard her laughing as she went up the stairs.

'Poor lassie,' said Mrs Macdonald. 'This has reminded her of her own father, who'll never come back. We shouldn't forget that she must be missing him terribly.'

Twenty-Nine

He had arranged to visit Aunt Fiona again at Easter. She had invited Sheila too but, with uncharacteristic stubbornness, surprising Mrs Macdonald, he had said that he would rather go alone. He had intended to search the machair for the boulder he had sat on when he had the encounter with the beetle and had discovered that he was one of the Chosen. It was a special miraculous place whose magic Sheila would have spoiled.

His visit had to be cancelled. Since his aunt was now in her cottage which had no telephone he had to write, explaining and apologising.

He didn't want to go to school, but Mrs Macdonald said he should. What if his father didn't come for another week or more? Matthew would miss too many lessons.

Every day he hurried home and dashed into the house, to be met by Mrs Macdonald sadly shaking her head.

He listened to the six o'clock news every evening and prayed that there would be no plane crashes.

'Do you know what they say about a watched kettle?' said Sheila. 'It never boils. Well, an expected father never comes.'

'That's silly.' But he felt another pang of foreboding.

She came into his room one evening and caught him on his knees, praying.

'Who are you praying to?' she asked, scornfully. 'Pegasus? You might as well.'

'I've been praying too,' she said. 'I've been praying that your father changes his mind and never comes home. Why shouldn't my prayer be answered?'

He thought he knew why. His was a good prayer, hers was wicked. Surely God preferred to answer good prayers. But there was always that tiny doubt that God was not always to be relied on. Sometimes the Devil was in the way.

Days passed without further news of his father.

'That's what you get for not wanting me to go to Uist with you,' said Sheila.

She was being sarcastic but perhaps she was right. Perhaps he was being punished. Just in case he went out of his way looking for kind things to do. He was especially kind to Lucy.

'Don't worry,' said Mrs Macdonald. 'He'll come. You've waited patiently for three years. Surely you can wait a week or two longer.'

'Sheila says he could have changed his mind.'

'Sheila had no right to say anything of the kind She's too fond of saying things like that.'

Mrs Macdonald had begun to notice Sheila's unkind re-marks.

Your father will come, thought Mrs Macdonald, being unkind herself, maybe not for your sake, son, but for his ain. Maybe he's not been able to sell his paintings and needs money.

Once, after tea, he went up to the studio and sat among the paintings, trying to remember his father. He remembered the black smock splattered with paint, and the little specks of paint on his father's beard. He had been allowed to watch his father working as long as he kept quiet. He had liked the smell of his father's cigar. The studio was the only place where his father

161

smoked. He hadn't known his father all that well, not nearly as well as he had known his mother. He had never shared secrets with him, the way he had with her. His father might look like a stranger. Matthew would be eager to hear about his adventures in Mexico and to see the pictures he had painted there.

Sheila entered without knocking. 'Why are you sitting in the dark?' She switched on the light.

'I've been thinking.'

She laughed. 'You can't think. You haven't got the brains. You're just a child.'

'I'm the same age as you.'

'I know hundreds of things you don't.'

She was prowling about, turning paintings so that she could see them.'

'They're awful. No wonder he went away so that he could learn to paint better.'

'They're not awful. Lots of people bought his paintings.'

'Is this supposed to be your mother?'

He shook his head. The woman's face was not unlike his mother's but his mother had never allowed herself to be painted with no clothes on.

'Did he love your mother?'

'Yes.'

'How do you know?'

'He went away when she died.'

'That doesn't mean anything. There's no such thing as love. Love for someone else, I mean. People just love themselves. You're not very bright but you must have noticed that. You're an example yourself. They all say what a nice little boy Matthew Sowglass is. You never hear him speak ill of anyone. But what is he really like? I'll tell you. He's selfish, like everybody else. He doesn't care for anyone but himself.'

She was saying it because he had refused to let her go to Uist with him.

But could it be true? Some boys at school called him stuck-up because he didn't swear and went to church. He hadn't any really close friend. Not even Davy Moore had been his close friend.

'You can't say your father loves you.'

'Yes, I can.'

'He went away and left you, didn't he? For three years. And he didn't write.'

'I told you why he went away.'

'Because your mother had died? But most people would say that was a reason why he should have stayed with you, or taken you with him. Ask Mrs Macdonald.'

Before he could find an answer they heard Mrs Macdonald shouting up the stairs.

'What's she saying?' he asked. But he knew. She was saying that his father was on the telephone.

He rushed out and went down the stairs pell-mell.

He passed Mrs Macdonald. 'Be careful,' she cried.

There was the telephone on the table under the stag's head. He had never thought of it as beautiful. Now he did. He lifted it reverently.

'It's me, Dad,' he screamed. 'Matthew. It's me.'

He had never heard himself scream before.

His father laughed, or rather the person at the other end laughed. Was it his father? It didn't sound like his father. But what would his father have sounded like?

'Where are you, Dad?' He was still screaming.

'Hey, take it easy, muchacho.'

'No, I'm Matthew.'

'Yes, I've gathered that. What age are you now, Matthew?'

Surely he should have known?

'Twelve. I'm twelve. Nearly thirteen.'

'You'll be at secondary school now?'

'Yes.'

'Lunderston High. Is old Pussyfoot still headmaster?'

That was Mr Shepherd's nickname. But what an unimportant thing to say, after so long a silence. Yet what did he expect his father to say? Things that couldn't be said.

'Where are you?'

'London.'

So he was safely over the ocean.

'When are you coming home?'

'Tomorrow.'

'Tomorrow!' Suddenly, after all those empty days of waiting, it seemed too soon. He wasn't ready. Sheila had said it would be a let-down. It mustn't be. He wouldn't let it be. 'Are you coming by train?'

'No, I'm flying. By the way, I've got a surprise for you, a big surprise.'

'What is it?'

'Now it wouldn't be a surprise, would it, if I told you what it was?'

'No.'

'What sort of weather are you having up there?'

Again, what an unimportant thing to say. But perhaps that was his father's way of saying he loved him.

'It's cold but it's not raining.'

'You must be joking. Isn't it always raining?'

'No, not always. It wasn't raining yesterday either.'

His father laughed. 'Well, let's hope it's not raining tomorrow. Good night, Matthew.'

'Good night, Dad.'

He put the telephone down, with great reluctance.

'Did he say when he was coming?' asked Mrs Macdonald.

'Tomorrow.'

'Yes, but when? In the morning or afternoon?'

'I don't think he said. He's flying. He said he had a surprise for me, a big surprise. He didn't say what it was.'

'Maybe it's a parrot.' Sheila had come down the stairs.

'A parrot?'

'Don't you know Mexico's famous for parrots?'

'Why would he bring me a parrot? It would have to go into quarantine, wouldn't it?'

She sneered. 'You never see a joke, do you?'

Was she confessing that her claims to have killed Davy Moore and her father had been jokes?

'I don't have to go to school tomorrow, do I?'

'Of course not,' said Mrs Macdonald.

'I'll stay off too,' said Sheila.

'You don't have to. Does she, Mrs Macdonald?'

'Maybe she should, to keep you company.'

If there was one person's company he did not want tomorrow it was Sheila's.

'Now I suppose I should get the house ready,' said Mrs Macdonald.

'I'll help later,' he said, and rushed upstairs to his room. He would lock the door to keep Sheila out.

He was in the kitchen doing homework, Mrs Macdonald was polishing the electric kettle, Lucy was asleep in front of the fire, and Sheila was playing the piano in the front room, when the telephone rang.

He rushed out. It might be his father again.

It was Aunt Fiona.

'Hello,' he said.

'Is that you, Matthew?'

'Yes, it's me. Have you got a telephone in the cottage now?'

'No. I'm telephoning from the hotel.'

How had she got there? Had she walked? It was more than a mile. It would be dark and there were no street lights. There were no streets. She would have to carry a torch. He hoped it

165

wasn't raining. If there were stars they would give her some light.

'Thank you for your letter.' She paused. 'You'll be very happy now that you've got your father home.'

'He's not here yet. He's coming tomorrow. He's in London. He says he's got a big surprise for me, but he didn't say what it was.'

'Whatever it is I'm sure it will be a very pleasant one.'

'Yes, I think so. Is your back better?'

'Much better, thank you.'

'Do you like living in the cottage?'

'Yes. The seals are very friendly.'

'Don't you feel lonely?'

His own loneliness would end tomorrow, so he felt hers all the more keenly. He imagined her standing on the shore, talking to the seals.

'Would you like me to come and visit you during the Easter holidays?'

'I would like that very much, Matthew. Well, good night. Please give my regards to Mrs Macdonald, and to your father.'

'Yes, I will. Good night.'

If his father still hated her he would tell him how much she had changed. Perhaps his father had changed too, in lots of ways.

Sheila had stopped playing the piano. She had been listening.

He went into the kitchen.

'Was that your aunt?' asked Mrs Macdonald.

'Yes. She wanted to tell me she got my letter. She said to give you her regards.'

'That was kind of her. I thought you said she didn't have a telephone?'

'She went to the hotel to telephone.'

He imagined his aunt walking bravely back, shining her torch.

'It's more than a mile away.'

'It'd be dark.'

'Oh yes, very dark. I said I'd like to visit her during the holidays. Do you think my father will let me?'

'I don't see why not.'

Mrs Macdonald hoped Sowglass wasn't coming home to give orders. He would have to earn the right to do that. It might take him some time.

Satisfied, Matthew sat down and resumed his homework.

Thirty

Next day, which was to be the happiest day of his life, rain battering against his bedroom window woke him early. He got up to look out. The clouds were almost at the level of the sea. Would planes be able to fly safely in such weather? What if they couldn't and his father didn't come till tomorrow, or the day after? It wouldn't matter much, it wouldn't be the end of everything, like death, he would still come, with his surprise.

There had been happy days before, when his mother was alive; but there had always been the threat of illness, and then illness itself, to spoil it all.

At breakfast he expected Sheila to jeer that bad weather caused plane crashes, but she kept quiet.

He couldn't eat, for excitement. He kept wanting to rush through to the front window to watch for the taxi.

'You'll make yourself sick,' said Mrs Macdonald.

'Do you think we should telephone the airport to see if planes are flying?'

'Later, maybe, if it gets any worse.'

They heard thunder. There must have been lightning. It was still quite dark outside.

Sheila got up and left the kitchen. They heard her going upstairs.

He didn't notice, but Mrs Macdonald went out and called after her, 'Are you all right, Sheila?'

'Yes, I'm all right.'

'She's jealous, that's what's the matter with her,' he cried. 'She doesn't want my father to come home.'

'That's a silly thing to say, Matthew.'

'But it's true. She said she prayed for him not to come home.'

'She was teasing you.'

'No, she meant it. You don't know her.'

'You're being foolish, Matthew, and not very nice. I would have thought your father coming home would have made you more sympathetic. *Her* father isn't coming home.'

'She doesn't want him to.'

'What a thing to say, Matthew Sowglass.'

'She said it wasn't an accident, in the boat. She said she pushed him. She told me she was going to do it.'

He was almost hysterical.

'I think, Matthew, you should take an aspirin and then go and lie down for a while. I hope you never say things like that to anyone else. I make allowances but other people might not. I wouldn't like to think that your father coming home is going to make you selfish and spiteful.'

She could see, though, how it might. His was a sensitive nature, easily damaged.

At eleven o'clock they telephoned and were assured that planes from London were arriving, just a few minutes late.

He stood at the front window, waiting and watching. Lucy, apparently aware of his unrest, came and rubbed against his legs. She would be glad to see his father. He had let her into his studio. He had said she would keep the mice away.

Sheila was staying in her room.

Mrs Macdonald went up once to see how she was.

169

'Do you know what the poor girl's doing?' she said, when she came back.

He wasn't interested.

'She's packing.'

He still wasn't interested.

'I told her not to be in too big a hurry. I'm sure your father won't mind her being here, especially when he learns how unlucky she's been. I hope, Matthew, you won't say to him the awful things you said to me.'

The truth was, Mrs Macdonald had become rather anxious. There was some instability in the boy's family, on his mother's side, due to too much religion. His Aunt Fiona, not so long ago a hard-hearted bitch, had become almost a saint, or so it seemed. Matthew was a deep little boy, keeping his thoughts to himself. The excitement of his father's return might make him ill, mentally as well as physically. She hoped his father would have the sense to handle the situation carefully. It didn't look like it, with his promise of a big surprise.

She herself would have to show restraint. She would be tempted to say something to Sowglass about his callousness in deserting his son, but she would wait until she was convinced that he was genuinely sorry. It wasn't her place, as a mere servant, to rebuke him, and it might cost her her job, but if he didn't make an honest effort to make it up to Matthew she wouldn't be able to hold her tongue.

Thirty-One

I t was after six when the taxi stopped outside the house. He was so exhausted and numb with watching that he didn't notice it till Mrs Macdonald yelled, 'That's him now.'

He didn't move. He couldn't. He was paralysed with expectation and joy.

'Aren't you going out to welcome him?' she cried, on her way to open the front door.

Slowly and stiffly he went and stood beside her on the top step.

It had stopped raining. The wet road gleamed in the lamplight. So did the taxi. The driver was already taking suitcases out of the boot. So far there was no sign of Sowglass. Then there he was, wearing a big hat, the kind called a sombrero. He got out and then reached in to bring out – a parrot? thought Mrs Macdonald, foolishly – no, a person wrapped in a cape, the kind called a poncho, that even in the lamplight was seen to be brightly coloured, like a parrot's feathers indeed . . . She was a woman, small and stout, with black hair.

She must be a servant he's brought with him, thought Mrs Macdonald, herself on the verge of hysteria.

Then she turned to Matthew. If the look of fury she had seen on Sheila's face had horrified her, this was worse, far worse. Hatred and despair disfigured him. He was almost unrecognisable. Was the hatred directed towards his father, or the woman, or both? Surely not his father, and the woman, whoever she was, had done him no harm.

Sowglass saw them at the door. 'Hello, there,' he cried, cheerfully.

'For God's sake, Matthew,' she muttered, 'whatever you're feeling hide it, hide it for now.'

She herself went down the steps, trying hard to smile.

'Mrs Macdonald,' he said, proudly, 'this is my wife, Conchita.'

So this was the big surprise.

'Pleased to meet you,' said Mrs Macdonald, and never had she told a bigger lie. But she took the hand that the woman timidly held out. Every finger seemed to have a ring, but she was by no means brazen. On the contrary she was very shy. Mrs Macdonald couldn't help being touched. It wasn't the poor creature's fault that she was there and besides, she was far from home. So Mrs Macdonald did her best to be hospitable, all the more so because Matthew was no longer there, he had fled into the house and she had caught a glimpse of him going up the stairs.

'You'll have to excuse him,' she said. 'It's been too much for him. He's been waiting since early morning. To tell the truth he's been waiting for three years.'

Sowglass laughed. 'He always was a funny little fellow.'

That nettled Mrs Macdonald. Talk about funny, she thought, what would you call this wife of yours?

How could a man who had been married to a pale, delicate, blue-eyed Hebridean beauty like Catriona McLure have chosen to replace her with this squat, heavy-faced, dark-skinned, Indian-looking creature who, to add to her unattractiveness, was obviously pregnant?

Mrs Macdonald was glad to take refuge in carrying one of

172

suitcases up the steps and into the hall. It was heavy, but a feather-weight compared to the burden on her mind. The home-coming, looked forward to for so long, had gone all wrong. She blamed Sowglass.

The taxi had gone. The driver had given Mrs Sowglass a last peculiar look. She would get plenty of those in Lunderston. Weren't artists supposed to be experts on the subject of beauty? Not modern ones, apparently. Look at the pictures of women Picasso had painted. Yes, but, from what she had read, Picasso had chosen attractive women to go to bed with.

You should be ashamed, Bella Macdonald, she told herself, as she helped the woman up the steps. There are more ways of being beautiful than having a well-shaped nose.

Sheila had come downstairs to greet them. She did it very graciously, as if making up for Matthew's rudeness.

'I'm Sheila Burnside,' she said. 'I'm staying here.'

The contrast between her fairness and the woman's darkness was painful, at least to Mrs Macdonald. Sowglass seemed unaware of it.

'I'll tell you about Sheila later,' said Mrs Macdonald.

'Is there still just the one bathroom?'

'Yes. There's also the downstairs toilet.'

Mrs Macdonald remembered that one of the effects of pregnancy was the need to go often and sometimes urgently.

Sowglass spoke to his wife in a foreign language, and then took her to the toilet at the back of the house.

Where she came from, thought Mrs Macdonald, had she an inside toilet, with a flush? Perhaps she was the daughter of a chief. She fairly tinkled and sparkled with jewellery: rings, bangles, necklaces, and earrings; nothing on her nose, though.

'Some surprise,' said Sheila.

Sowglass came back. He had taken off his hat. His hair, bleached by the sun, was fairer than Sheila's. His beard too.

'Where's Matthew got to?' he asked.

'I think he's upstairs in his room. He doesn't mean to be rude. He's just over-excited.'

Then Sowglass caught sight of Lucy, who had come into the hall, tail up, thoroughly at home.

He couldn't have been more alarmed if she'd been a tiger.

'I forgot about her. She'll have to go. Conchita's allergic to cats. They make her eyes water and cause her to cough.'

'Matthew's had Lucy for years.'

'Yes, I know. It's a pity, but we'll have to get rid of her. Now, I mean, before Conchita comes back.'

Sheila picked up the cat and took her into the kitchen.

Mrs Sowglass came back. Almost at once her eyes watered.

'There's a cat,' said Sowglass.' We'll have to get rid of it. What room have you put us in, Mrs Macdonald?'

'Your old room.'

'Thank you.'

He cleeked his wife tenderly up the stairs.

'There's a meal ready when you are. A real Scotch high tea.'

It was a feast that was laid out in the dining-room, with Mrs Macdonald's own baking and the best cold meat that Lunderston could supply. The best delf and cutlery were to be used.

Mrs Macdonald remembered having read somewhere that there were injections which could cure that particular allergy. But were they given to the cat or to the person affected?

It would be her who would have to tell Matthew that his cat would have to be got rid of.

She felt angry with Sowglass and not with the woman. There he was, with his purple trousers and red socks, taking over the house as if he hadn't, by his long absence, forfeited his right.

Sheila came into the hall. She was grinning. 'What a horrible creature!'

'She's not horrible. Watch your tongue, young lady. Just because she's different doesn't mean she's horrible.'

'She's different all right. She's pregnant, isn't she?'

The young besom missed nothing.

'Not only is Matthew going to have his cat put down, he's also going to have a wee nigger for his stepbrother or stepsister.'

That made Mrs Macdonald angry. 'Do you have to say such nasty things?'

'They may be nasty, Mrs Macdonald, but they're true.'

'I advise you to say nothing; that's to say, if you want to stay on in this house. It's under new management.'

Mrs Macdonald then, with a sigh that had exasperation in it, went upstairs to talk to Matthew.

She knocked on his door, quietly. She didn't want his father to appear. This was between her and Matthew. He was more her son, and her responsibility, than Sowglass's. Or so she felt. She had a right to talk sternly to him, if it was needed.

'Who is it?' he asked.

'Me. Mrs Macdonald.'

He opened the door.

She had hoped that he would have got over the initial shock, and so he had, to some degree. There was no longer despair on his face, only hatred.

She hardly recognised him. Where was the boy who everybody praised for his patience and politeness?

And this was before he had been told he had to get rid of his cat.

She sat down, feeling weak. The big hobby-horse stared at her contemptuously with its yellow eyes. What use are you, it seemed to be saying.

She made a great effort. She remembered she loved him.

'I know this has been a big shock to you, Matthew. It's

been a big shock to me too. But we'll have to be brave about it.'

'Who is she?'

'She's your father's new wife.'

'But who is she? Where did he find her? She looks like a savage.'

'She's Mexican. Lots of Mexicans are part Spanish, part Indian.'

'Has she come to take my mother's place?'

'I don't think she thinks that.'

God knew what the outlandish creature thought. Why, in God's name, had Sowglass married her? She was hardly the kind of woman a man would want to sleep with. There must have been many handsomer than she.

'Does my father think she can take my mother's place?'

But, Matthew, your mother doesn't count. She's out of the game.

Be fair, though. Perhaps Sowglass loved her and she, in her mysterious way, loved him.

Mrs Macdonald remembered she was a servant, with duties to attend to.

She got up. 'Are we going down to have our tea?'

'I don't want any.'

'All right. I'll bring you up something.'

'I'd like Sheila to bring it up.'

This was odd. Usually he tried to avoid being beholden to Sheila. 'I'll ask her.'

'Tell her I want to talk to her.'

'I'll tell her.'

Mrs Macdonald went out, feeling defeated.

She chapped, respectfully, on Sowglass's door. She was just the housekeeper.

He opened it, with his finger at his lips. 'Conchita's asleep. She was very tired.'

'She won't be wanting her tea then?'

'Perhaps she'll have something later. Have you spoken to Matthew?'

'Yes.'

'Do you think I should have a word with him myself?'

She was astonished at his asking. 'Yes, I think you should!' Not wishing to say any more in the meantime she excused herself and went downstairs.

After making sure that Conchita was asleep, Sowglass closed the door quietly and went to knock on Matthew's. He did feel a little conscience-stricken: he had been away too long and he could have written oftener; but then he had been so busy painting and had produced so many successful pictures, that he had found it easy to forgive himself, and he could see no reason why Matthew shouldn't forgive him too, though the forgiveness of a twelve-year-old hardly mattered. Especially a twelve-year-old who didn't feel things all that deeply. He hadn't shed a tear at his mother's death. It could simply be lack of intelligence, but it was also a consequence of his having crazy Calvinism instilled in him from the very cradle, by his mother, his dreadful aunts, and his unforgiving grandfather.

It was certainly a rather wandered-looking little fellow that came to the door, one who would have difficulty in understanding and accepting the new conditions in his life. Sowglass had hoped, with not much confidence it was true, that Matthew would appreciate his paintings with their bold colours, not as a critic of course but as a son proud of his father's achievements. Now he saw that that was unlikely. This was evidently a boy without much imagination. It was a pity but not a surprise. Not only in looks did he take after his mother's side. Sowglass had loved her but she had never admired his work. He hadn't blamed her but it had caused a certain diminution.

'I see you've still got Pegasus,' he said, as he went into the room. It was he who had given the hobby-horse its name. 'Aren't you a bit old for it?' It was the wrong thing to say, but then he had never been good at finding the right things.

Matthew said nothing. He never had had much to say.

'I'm sorry about Lucy,' said Sowglass.

'Lucy?'

'Yes, I'm afraid she'll have to go.'

'Go? Go where?'

'To a new home. You see, Matthew, Conchita's allergic to cats. They make her ill.'

'Allergic?'

'It seems to be their fur. Her eyes water and she can't stop coughing if a cat comes near her.'

'I don't want Lucy to go.'

'I'm sure you don't, but people are more important than cats, aren't they? Conchita doesn't keep well. She's to be very careful about her health. She's not used to cold.'

It was like talking to a cat. The boy didn't seem to understand half of what was said to him. It was obvious that he had been pampered by Mrs Macdonald.

'If Lucy has to go I'll go too.'

'There's no need for that. This is your home.'

'It's my house.'

Sowglass frowned. What mischief-maker had told him that? Mrs Macdonald? What else had she told him? Not only Lucy might have to go.

'It's both our homes, Matthew.'

'Are you going to go away again?'

Sowglass laughed. 'Well, eventually. I can't see myself stuck in Lunderston for the rest of my life, and Conchita needs a warm climate. Next time, though, you can come with me, if you wanted.'

Matthew shook his head.

'Now why don't we go down and eat the food that Mrs Macdonald has prepared for us.'

'I don't want any.'

'Please yourself.' Sowglass wasn't going to argue or cajole. This huff was a childish reaction. 'So it looks as if it'll just be me and that girl Sheila. Conchita's sound asleep. Maybe you and she can get something to eat later.'

Matthew nodded.

It'll be all right, decided Sowglass, amused, he'll come round, he'll give no trouble.

'By the way' he said, 'how are you getting on at school?'

'All right.'

'What class have they put you in?'

'1A.'

Sowglass was taken aback. He had expected 1D. 1A was for the cleverest pupils.

Not only Matthew was in a huff. So, it seemed, was Mrs Macdonald. She wasn't going to eat with them in the dining-room. She would eat in the kitchen. She knew her place. She was a servant paid for what she did.

Sowglass knew what was the matter. *She* hadn't forgiven him. She had a damned cheek. It was none of her business. Yes, she would have to go, once Conchita had settled in.

She had, though, prepared an excellent meal. Sowglass had never been much interested in food, except as a subject for a still-life painting. To give her her due Mrs Macdonald had prepared an excellent meal: a genuine Scottish high tea: her own baking, three kinds of Scottish cold meats, including potted hough, and bramble jelly. The brambles, she said, had been gathered by herself and Matthew in the Afton woods. He had himself gathered brambles there long ago.

He ate with an enjoyment that surprised him. He hadn't realised that coming home would mean so much to him, at least in the beginning. He wasn't sure what his position would be. Not only the house but the shop and the money in the bank weren't his, but Matthew's. Grandfather Sowglass in his will had seen to that. 'I'll tell you why, Hugh. I wouldn't be dead six months before you'd sold everything and left the town for good. You've always hated Lunderston.' It was true enough. He'd particularly disliked the High School. Though he'd won prizes for drawing he had always been put in lower classes, like 1C. To be fair, he had neglected all other subjects in favour of Art. In Lunderston High, as in most other Scottish schools, Art was of little importance. It didn't qualify you for a good steady job.

He became aware that he was being stared at by a pair of shrewd young eyes. They belonged to the girl Sheila.

At last she had her questions ready. 'Did you paint a lot of pictures when you were in Mexico, Mr Sowglass?'

If there was a subject he didn't mind talking about it was his paintings. 'Quite a lot.'

'Why haven't you brought them back with you?'

'They've been sent direct to a gallery in Edinburgh. They're going to be on show there. I've already sold some in Mexico City and New York.'

'Did you get good prices?'

That was an impertinent question for a twelve-year-old to ask; for anyone, in fact. But because he was able to answer it affirmatively he didn't mind. 'Yes, I did.'

Suddenly he was overwhelmed by a surge of self-confidence. This inquisitive girl didn't matter. No one did. Not even Matthew. Not even Conchita, God forgive him. Only his painting mattered. He knew how good he was. He had shown them and he would show them again. He was still young. His was a talent too big for Scotland, far less an obscure little town like Lunderston.

'You won't be staying here for the rest of your life,' she said.

ed the committee had never asked him to contribute. They had known better.

'I suppose for them it's a harmless hobby,' he said.

He wasn't being condescending. He had a talent, perhaps a genius, but he had had to suffer for it. So had Catriona, and poor little Matthew.

He would let nothing stand in his way; not even Conchita's pregnancy. He had suggested an abortion but she had been horrified. But really it wasn't so very important. The child would probably die at birth or soon after. Whether it lived or died Conchita's primitive inspirations would be intensified, not diminished. He owed a lot to them.

'I've seen your pictures in the studio,' said persistent Sheila.

He grinned. 'I hope you approved of them.'

'One doesn't approve of a picture, does one? I mean, one either likes it or not.'

He was surprised. She certainly was an exceptional young lady.

'I liked the one called *Saligo Bay*.'

Again he was surprised. There was as much ancient menace in that picture as in those painted in Mexico. He had walked those sands with Catriona. He remembered a dead gannet.

They were interrupted by Mrs Macdonald.

'If you're finished, Sheila, would you take this tray up to Matthew.'

'Why doesn't he come down?' asked Sowglass.

She tried to keep her temper. 'You shouldn't have to ask that, Mr Sowglass. He needs time.'

'Time for what?'

'Time to adjust. Maybe it's not my place, Mr Sowglass, I'm just a servant here, but I have to say what's in my mind. You were very wrong to stay away so long. You could have done the child great damage for the rest of his life. Maybe you have. That's what I think. It's what the whole town thinks.'

'The whole town can mind its own damned business.'

'People in Lunderston take an interest in one another, Mr Sowglass.'

'That's one way to describe parochial nosiness.'

Provoked, Mrs Macdonald made a decision. She was going to tell a lie.

'I hope you'll have no objection to Matthew going to Uist at Easter. It's all arranged.'

Sheila was amused. It had been arranged but it had been cancelled.

'What's he going to Uist for?'

'To spend a holiday with his aunt Fiona.'

'That iron-hearted bitch!'

'She's changed. Three years is a long time, Mr Sowglass. A body can change a lot in three years. She's become fond of him and he of her.'

'From what I remember of her treatment of him when his mother died I find that hard to believe. She wasn't very friendly to you either, if I remember rightly. You must be more forgiving than me. What about the old man?'

'He's dead. Do you think, Sheila, you'll manage that?'

Smiling, Sheila picked up the tray. The next day or two were going to be very interesting.

Thirty-Two

The door wasn't just shut, it was locked. Who was the little fool trying to hide from? She kicked it with her foot. 'It's me, Sheila. I've brought you some food.'

She wouldn't have been surprised if he hadn't heeded her, but he came at once and opened the door. Never before had he looked eager to see her.

He pushed past her, as if to make sure there was no one about, and then came in and locked the door again.

'She's asleep,' he hissed.

Sheila put down the tray. 'Who's asleep?'

'Her. That woman.'

'You mean your stepmother?'

'She's not my stepmother.'

'If she's married to your father she is.'

'He shouldn't have married her.'

'Well, he did.'

'He shouldn't have brought her here.'

'Well, he has. How do you know she's asleep?'

'I went in and looked.'

'You went into her room?'

'It's not her room.'

'Well, it's the one she was put into. Why did you go in and look?'

'I wanted to kill her.'

Sheila laughed. 'Is that all?'

'It would have been easy but I didn't have a knife or anything.'

Her feelings towards him as a would-be murderer were akin to those of his father towards the members of the Art Club as artists.

'If you don't think she's your stepmother what do you think she is?'

'A cunt. She's a cunt.'

'Like Miss Johnston?'

'She's worse than Miss Johnston. I hate her.'

'How can you hate her if you don't know her?'

'You said you hated everybody and you don't know everybody.'

'That was different.'

'I hate her because she's trying to take my mother's place.'

'All right, you hate her and you want to kill her. How are you going to do it without being found out and sent to prison for twenty years?'

'They can't send me to prison.'

'Because you're just twelve? If you're over eight you can be sent to prison. That's the law.'

'They can't.'

'Why can't they?'

'It's a secret.'

She wondered if the shock of seeing the woman had damaged his brain.

'I don't know if I can tell you.'

'Tell me what?'

'There are people who can't be punished whatever they do. God protects them. They're called the Elect. That means Chosen. God chose them, in the beginning.'

'The beginning of what?'

184

'Of the world.'

She was sure now he was crazy or just childish; which was the same thing.

'How do they know they're chosen? Who tells them?'

'They just know.'

'Was it your daft old grandfather who told you this?'

'Yes, but he wasn't daft.'

'Who told him?'

'It's in the Bible.'

'Supposing there are such people, just supposing, how do you know you're one of them?'

She spoke contemptuously, and yet she liked the idea. If there were such people she was more likely to be one than he.

'Because of a beetle, a small green beetle.'

She was astonished. 'A beetle?'

'I killed it and it came alive again.'

'Where did this happen?'

'In the Hebrides.'

Where, she thought, they still believed in fairies.

He came close. 'I want you to help me.'

'To do what?'

'Kill her. Get rid of her.'

'Why do you think I can help you?'

'Because you killed Davy Moore and your father and the baby in the pram, and I didn't tell on you.'

'You said those were stupid lies. Do you still think they were stupid lies?'

He shook his head.

'All right. Why don't we do it now?'

'Now?'

'Why not? She's asleep. Your father's gone up to his studio. Mrs Macdonald's in the kitchen.'

'How will we do it?

'That's for you to decide. I'm just your helper.'

'We could put a pillow over her face. What your father did to your mother.'

'Who told you that?'

'You did.'

'Did I? Do you believe everything you're told?'

'I can't do it alone.'

'Go and see if she's still asleep. That's the first thing.'

He crept out and soon was back, looking disappointed and yet relieved. 'She's awake.'

'Did she see you?'

'I don't think so. She's still in bed. She had something in her hand. She was talking to it.'

'What was it?'

'I didn't see it.'

'It would be a crucifix. She's a Catholic. They all have crucifixes.'

His grandfather had called Catholics anti-Christs, whatever that meant.

'She would be praying,' said Sheila.

He nodded. It had sounded like prayer.

'What if God's on her side?'

He nodded. He didn't trust God. God was easily deceived. If she prayed with a crucifix in her hand maybe God would give her whatever it was she was praying for.

'You'll just have to wait,' said Sheila. 'Anyway, there's no great hurry, is there?'

Yes, there was. If it was put off too long he might not want to do it. He would never like the woman but he might stop hating her.

Thirty-Three

Now that he had made up his mind to get rid of his stepmother and so have his father to himself he found it quite easy to face her and even let her talk to him in a friendly way. Sheila encouraged him by whispering into his ear that if he was nice to his stepmother now he wouldn't be suspected afterwards. Knowing, however, how soft-hearted he was and how he liked people to like him, she warned him not to become too fond of his stepmother. Not that that need prevent him from getting rid of her. People more often than not murdered not those they hated but those they loved: that was human nature. In his case it wouldn't be murder, it would just be getting rid of a nuisance.

As if she was part of the plot Mrs Macdonald kept urging him to be kind to his stepmother. To that end she often praised her; which was easy enough to do without lying or exaggerating, for the stout young Mexican woman soon showed herself to be good-natured, grateful, and anxious to please; and also, to Mrs Macdonald's secret relief, very clean in her habits. Coming more or less out of the jungle she might have been expected to be, well, a bit smelly, but no, on the contrary, she was never out of the bathroom and washed her hair every day, so that Mrs Macdonald wondered if it had something to do with her religion.

She kept saying how sorry she was about Lucy. According to Sheila this was slyness, but he didn't think so. She told him about pets she had had: these included a parrot. He listened politely.

He had written to Aunt Fiona, saying that after all he and Sheila would like to visit her at Easter and that, if she didn't mind, they would bring Lucy with them. He explained about his stepmother's allergy. If Aunt Fiona liked Lucy perhaps she would keep her.

His aunt replied by telephone. She had again walked to the hotel.

He was able to speak freely. His father had gone to Edinburgh, Conchita was upstairs in the bathroom, and Sheila was playing the piano.

'Good evening, Matthew. Thank you for your letter.'

'Are you speaking from the hotel?'

'Yes.'

'Did you walk?'

'Yes, I walked.'

'I hope it's a nice night.'

'Yes, it is. The stars are shining.'

He pictured her carefully avoiding the pot holes.

'Good. Is it all right for me and Sheila to come?'

'Of course it is. I'll be delighted to see you.'

'Is it all right if we bring Lucy?'

'Yes, of course, but wouldn't it be better to find a home for her in Lunderston? If she's here you wouldn't be able to see her very often.'

'Mrs Macdonald's tried, but people say Lucy's too old, they prefer kittens. You'll like her. She's very friendly and she's good at catching mice.'

'As long as the gulls don't catch her.'

'Will they try to?'

'I'm sure she'll be too smart for them. You must be very happy now that your father's home.'

Sheila had stopped playing. She would be listening.

'Yes, but I didn't think he'd bring someone with him.'

'Was that the big surprise?'

'Yes. She's a Mexican.'

'I don't think I've ever met a Mexican. Can she speak English?'

'Yes, but she and my father speak to each other in Spanish. She's a Catholic.'

He was sure Aunt Fiona like his grandfather wouldn't approve of Catholics, but she just said, 'She would be, coming from Mexico.'

'She used to have a parrot that could talk. In Spanish.'

'She sounds very nice. I hope you're doing your best to make her feel at home.'

'Yes.' But he didn't say why.

'I think you'll be good at it. You have that kind of fortunate nature.'

He could tell she meant she herself didn't.

'I'm looking forward to seeing you and your friend.'

'And Lucy.'

'Of course, and Lucy. Your father doesn't mind you coming, does he?'

His father did mind but had kept quiet about it; because, Mrs Macdonald thought, Conchita had asked him to. 'She likes you, Matthew, and she wants you to like her.'

At Easter his father would be in Edinburgh to supervise the exhibition of his paintings. Conchita would be left in Mrs Macdonald's care. Mrs Macdonald was going to take her with her when she went shopping. 'We can't hide the poor soul away,' she said, resolutely. In fact she was rather looking forward to the sensation Conchita would cause, especially if she was wearing that parrot-like poncho.

189

Thirty-Four

M rs Macdonald drove them to Glasgow airport. It was a dull, cold, wet day. She felt guilty about leaving Conchita in the house by herself. Sowglass had gone to Edinburgh to see about his paintings.

'If you ask me he thinks more of his paintings than he does of her.'

'He has to,' said Sheila.

Matthew was seated in the back, with Lucy in her basket on his lap.

'What do you mean, Sheila?' asked Mrs Macdonald indignantly. 'She's his wife, for heaven's sake. He's supposed to love her above everything else.'

'If he's going to be a great painter he'll have to put his painting first.'

'Before his family?'

Matthew murmured to Lucy who was mewing sadly.

'Before everybody.'

'He'd have to be very good to justify that.'

'He'd have to be great.'

Matthew knew that Sheila had vowed to be a great singer one day.

'Well, I don't agree,' said Mrs Macdonald. 'His family should come first.'

'Who cares about Rembrandt's family? Or Maria Callas's?'

'Who's she?'

'A famous opera singer.'

'Well, I still think people should come first. Anyway, he should never have brought her to this cold country. She'll never thrive here.'

'Will she take pneumonia?' asked Matthew.

'Don't be so cheery, Matthew. More like TB.'

'What's that?'

'Tuberculosis.'

'Can you die of tuberculosis?'

'Yes, you can. Millions have died of it.'

Lucy mewed again, as if to tell him she shared his hope that his stepmother died of tuberculosis.

'What I don't understand', said Sheila, 'is why he brought *her*. There must have been lots of Mexican women more beautiful.'

'She was the one he loved.'

That was Isabel Macdonald, the romanticist, speaking, though in any romantic novel Conchita would have been the faithful servant, never the graceful heroine.

'No wonder they say love's blind,' said Sheila.

'That's not a nice thing to say, Sheila.'

'If she has a baby what colour will it be?'

'Why do you say "if"? Of course he's going to have a baby. What difference will it make what colour it is?'

'I don't think Matthew would like a wee black sister. Would you, Matthew?'

He pretended not to be listening.

'It won't be black,' said Mrs Macdonald. 'Conchita's not black.'

'She's very dark. It's funny, Mr Sowglass, so fair himself, choosing someone so dark.'

'People are often attracted to their opposites.'

'Was Mr Macdonald tall and slim?'

'Mr Macdonald? Oh, you mean my Angus. No, he wasn't tall and slim.'

'So he wasn't your opposite?'

Mrs Macdonald smiled, in the way she did when beaten at draughts. 'Looks don't matter in the end. Kindness is mair important. He was very kind.'

'Didn't you have a little girl?'

There was a photograph on the mantelpiece of Mrs Macdonald's room off the kitchen. It showed Mrs Macdonald with a little girl on her lap. A small man with a moustache was standing beside her.

'What happened to her?'

'She died.'

'What age was she?'

'Three.'

'What did she die of?'

'A fever.'

'What was her name?'

'Anabel.'

'Was that your mother's name?'

'My mither was called Jean.'

'Where did you get it, then. The name.'

'Out of a book.'

Sheila was silent and then she said, quietly: 'I'm very sorry, Mrs Macdonald.'

'It's all right, Sheila. It was a long time ago. But thanks just the same.'

Matthew thought, angrily: she's really laughing at you, Mrs Macdonald. But when Sheila turned to look at him he saw that her sadness and pity weren't feigned. He hardly recognised her.

Thirty-Five

'It's a nuisance, your aunt not having a telephone,' said Mrs Macdonald at the airport as she was saying goodbye.

'We'll go to the hotel and phone,' said Matthew. 'It's not far.'

'You do that. Every second night, if you can manage. About seven o'clock. Sheila, make sure he remembers.'

'I don't need Sheila to remind me.'

'Don't worry, Mrs Macdonald, I'll look after him.'

'I don't need anyone to look after me.'

Mrs Macdonald laughed. 'That's right, son, you don't. Be sure and give my regards to your aunt.'

'The iron-hearted bitch.' Sheila whispered it, but Mrs Macdonald heard. 'I hope that's not going to be your attitude, Sheila. If it is you'd better not go.'

'Wasn't that what Mr Sowglass called her?'

'What he called her's none of your business. She's been very kind inviting you.'

'I was just joking.'

'Not a nice joke, Sheila. Well, I hope poor Lucy settles in.'

Then off they went to board the plane. Lucy was already aboard, in her basket in the hold.

It was the same stewardess. She greeted them cheerfully.

'Hello there. Is this your sister?'

He shook his head.

'Ah, your girlfriend?'

'That's right,' said Sheila, smiling. 'I'm his girlfriend.'

'Well, I must say he's got good taste.'

Looks might not matter, but Sheila always used hers to her best advantage. On the plane she attracted admiring smiles, which she pretended not to notice. They would say, those passengers, that on the plane they had seen a lovely young girl who, though cheerful, had in the midst of her cheerfulness, a trace of sadness, that hadn't spoiled her loveliness but rather had enhanced it. She was with a boy, either her brother or her cousin, whom she had looked after attentively: he hadn't looked as grateful as he should. Perhaps they had had a bereavement in their family recently.

Aunt Fiona, waiting in misty Benbecula, saw, coming off the plane, in front of Matthew, a girl tall for her age, almost as tall as Aunt Fiona herself, with splendid long fair hair and a smile so bright that it made up for the absence of sunshine. She was, thought Aunt Fiona, the kind of daughter any woman would have been proud of and that Aunt Fiona herself had now and then let herself dream of having. In the airport Aunt Fiona felt like weeping, for profounder reasons than self-pity.

She was a girl with manners too. She waited till Matthew came and introduced her. Then she shook hands with Aunt Fiona and Dugald, the taxi-driver. Dugald had been warned that the girl coming with Matthew had not long ago lost her father in a yachting accident and so was now fatherless and motherless. Yet here she was, not only cheerful herself but ready to make others cheerful too. He sang her praises to his wife that night.

Poor little Matthew did his best, with his shy smiles and politeness, but beside Sheila he was hardly noticed.

When they collected Lucy in her basket she was still sound asleep, having been sedated.

Dugald and Aunt Fiona too would have been astonished and horrified if they had been able to read Matthew's thoughts.

He was imagining Sheila lurking in Puddock Lane, with the half brick in her hand. Davy was whistling as he approached, to give himself courage. She sprang out of the shadows and struck, once, twice, three times. Davy hadn't even time to shout before his face was a mess of blood and his head a mess of bone. She had no pity on her face as she dropped the half brick and stepped over the body.

Then she was strolling along the street in Glasgow. She looked about her, made sure no one was watching, stooped, released the brake, and gave the pram a push. It gathered speed as it rolled downhill. It left the pavement and ran into the path of a car. The baby was thrown out. Someone rushed towards it. There was blood on the street. Sheila watched and smiled.

With the sea so close to the road it was easy to imagine her in the yacht giving her father a sudden push. She was strong and he had been a small man. There he was struggling amidst the big waves, in his yellow life-jacket. Deceiving herself, for there was no one else to deceive, except her father himself, she pretended to make frantic efforts to save him. He was swept away towards the rocks. Her hair was soaked. She was laughing.

Had it all really happened? Previously he had thought it ridiculous lies. Now he wanted to believe that she had been telling the truth. He wanted her to be a murderer because he needed her help to get rid of his stepmother. He would never be able to do it by himself.

He *had* to get rid of his stepmother, not just for his own sake but also for his father's. It would be like curing his father of a terrible disease.

Meanwhile Sheila was letting Aunt Fiona and Dugald know that she was a good singer. She wasn't boasting. She hadn't volunteered the information. Aunt Fiona and Dugald had been talking about a ceilidh that was going to take place soon. One of the principal singers, a coastguard's wife, had been afflicted by a sore throat and wouldn't be able to perform. Dugald had asked, jocularly, if Sheila had any experience of singing: he was prepared to credit her with every talent. She had had to answer truthfully. She hastened to add that she didn't know Gaelic. Scots songs would do, said Dugald. Did she know any? Yes, she did. But as a stranger did she have a right to take part? Sure she had, visitors were often roped in.

'You're here on holiday,' said Aunt Fiona, but she was pleased.

She was pleased again when, after Dugald had set them down at the cottage, Sheila cried out with delight at its situation, which would have dismayed most people from a town, because of its isolation and its closeness to the sea. She picked up a bit of peat, shaped like a brick and held it in her hand as if, thought Matthew, it was a weapon, or as if, thought Aunt Fiona, she understood how precious peat was, how God-given, since it was a source of heat during the long dark cold winter.

Inside the cottage nothing disappointed her. Her bedroom was poky with a low sloped ceiling, but she didn't mind that because of the view, seaward, rocks with cormorants on them and seals. Remembering how she had spoken with glee about the swans' bloody feathers and how she had wantonly smashed the hedge-sparrow's eggs Matthew found it hard to believe that her pleasure at seeing those wild creatures was genuine. Not for the first time he wondered if she deceived not only other people but herself too. Was it a consequence of some mental illness?

She soon showed how sane, how frighteningly sane, she could be.

She came into his room which was as small as hers. Its view was of the machair.

She sat on the bed. 'Something's bothering me,' she said.

'What?'

'Your aunt's not well off.'

He made no comment.

'She's very poor.'

Again he said nothing.

'The taxi-driver didn't charge her the full amount.'

He had noticed that too. 'Why are you saying this?'

'I think we ought to pay for our keep.'

Mrs Macdonald and he had discussed what should be done about paying for Lucy's keep.

'Don't you agree?'

'Yes.' But he didn't see how it could be done without hurting his aunt's feelings.

'Will you mention it to her? You're her nephew.'

'I don't like to.'

'All right. I'll do it.'

'When?'

'Shouldn't we wait and ask Mrs Macdonald?'

'It's got nothing to do with Mrs Macdonald. Will you back me up?'

He nodded.

They heard his aunt calling that lunch was ready.

They went downstairs.

'Is the cat all right?' asked Aunt Fiona.

'She's under my bed,' said Matthew. 'I'll talk to her later. She knows my voice.'

Lunch consisted of home-made broth, Uist potatoes and mutton, and rice pudding.

'Nothing fancy, I'm afraid,' said Aunt Fiona.

Matthew noticed a small darn in the sleeve of his aunt's cardigan. There were other evidences of the need for thrift.

She had no rings. He remembered his stepmother had eight. He had counted them.

He waited with dread for Sheila to bring up the subject of money.

He knew she detested rice pudding but she was eating it as if she was enjoying it.

'Thank you for a delicious meal, Miss McLure,' she said.

His aunt smiled faintly. 'I'm afraid it was very ordinary.'

'Matthew and I would like to discuss something with you.'

His aunt sat very straight. He wondered if her back was painful.

Sheila put on her nicest smile. 'We want you to promise not to be offended. Don't we, Matthew?'

He wanted to run upstairs and hide under his bed with Lucy.

'We would be terribly sorry if you felt offended. Wouldn't we, Matthew?'

He had to nod. He couldn't look at his aunt.

'Do you promise, Miss McLure?'

'How can I promise without knowing what it is?'

'Please trust us.'

'Very well, I trust you.'

'We think it's only fair that we should pay for Lucy's keep and our own. Me, especially. I'm not a member of your family, like Matthew. I pay for my keep in Lunderston.'

They waited then for her answer. He couldn't bear it.

She carefully folded her napkin. She looked at it, not at them. Her fingers were a little clumsy. They heard birds screaming outside.

They were interrupted by Lucy who crept in, nervous and cautious. She looked at them and then made for her dishes in the kitchen.

'But you are my guests,' said his aunt. 'I invited you.'

'You would be doing us a great favour. Isn't that so, Matthew?'

He nodded, miserably.

His aunt rose. 'May I think about it?'

They rose too.

'I hope you're not offended,' said Sheila.

'No, I'm not offended. Why should kindness offend me? Besides, I have to learn to be humble.'

Though it was said quietly, still with a little smile, it was charged with bitterness, or was it sadness?

'Excuse me, please.' She went into the kitchen.

In a minute she was back again and stood in the doorway. She was very pale. 'I too have something to say. To you, Matthew. I'm sorry I was so unkind to your mother and to you when she died. I regret it every day. I do not expect you to believe me, you are right not to believe me, she would not have believed me, but of all my sisters I loved her the most. Why then did I not show it? I cannot tell you that, except to say it seemed to be my nature.'

She went back into the kitchen and closed the door.

'How was she unkind to your mother?' asked Sheila.

He shook his head. He didn't want to talk about it. He would never all his life talk about it.

'Was that why your father called her an iron-hearted bitch?'

He listened at the kitchen door but couldn't hear his aunt crying, thank goodness. Yet wouldn't it be better if she could cry? Mrs Macdonald had said that about him; so had his father long ago, when his mother had died. The McLures never cry, his father had said, sarcastically. But his mother had been a McLure and she had cried.

'Let's go to the hotel and hire bikes,' said Sheila.

And he could telephone Mrs Macdonald and tell her they had arrived safely.

Thirty-Six

I t was dry now and the sun was coming out. It glinted on the sea. Larks sang above them. Thinking of his aunt, unhappy in the kitchen with Lucy, who was unhappy too, he thought that he should change his mind and not try to get rid of his stepmother. He was sorry now that he had asked Sheila to help him.

Sheila was strangely elated. She looked up at the bright sky, seeking out the larks. She took long deep breaths. She laughed for joy. She was very happy. He expected her to say something kind about his aunt. He felt affection for her.

Suddenly she stopped and stood gazing at him.

'What she said about loving your mother, you didn't believe it, did you? She had to say it. She's a hypocrite. She can't help it. Everybody's a hypocrite. You know what a hypocrite is, don't you?'

'Not everybody.'

'Who's an exception then?'

'Mrs Macdonald.'

'Oh, who cares about her? She's old and stupid.'

'No, she isn't. Mrs Moore, Davy's mother. She always says what she thinks. She tells the truth.'

'She's scruff. What about yourself? You're one of the worst.

200

When you go home you'll be nice to your stepmother while all the time you're planning to kill her.'

'No, I'm not. Not any more.'

She didn't seem surprised. She sneered. 'I knew you'd never be able to go through with it. You're a coward.'

She went on then, dancing and singing. She stepped deliberately into pot holes full of water. 'Coward, coward, coward,' she sang. 'Don't think though that you're going to get out of it.'

He felt afraid. She was mad and he was the only one who knew.

There was no one using the telephone at the hotel.

Sheila stood very close to him.

'It's me, Matthew.'

'Why hello, Matthew,' said Mrs Macdonald. 'I didn't expect a call till this evening.'

'We had to come to the hotel to hire bikes.'

'I see. Did you have a nice flight?'

'Very nice, thanks. The stewardess remembered me.'

'I'm sure she did. How's Lucy settling in?'

'All right, I think. She hid under my bed but she came out to eat.'

'If she's eating then she feels at home. How is your aunt?'

That was more difficult to answer, especially with Sheila staring at him.

'Sheila and me asked her if she would mind if we paid for our keep.'

'Did you, indeed? Was it Sheila's idea?'

'Yes, but I agreed. My aunt's very poor, isn't she?'

'I don't expect your grandfather left her much. What did she say?'

'She didn't say very much.'

'No wonder. She'd be insulted. You're her guests.'

'That's what she said. But guests sometimes pay, don't they? She said she'd think about it. She said she'd have to learn to be humble.'

'You've humiliated her.'

'I didn't mean to.'

'I know that, son, but I'm not so sure about Sheila.'

Sheila seized the telephone. 'But, Mrs Macdonald, she needs the money.'

'Maybe she needs her pride more.'

'I don't think so. She really does want to learn to be humble. She apologised to Matthew for being unkind to him when his mother died.'

There was a pause.

'I suppose you meant well.'

'I was sorry for her, that's all.'

'Yes, Sheila, but you've got to be careful how you show it.'

Sheila handed Matthew the telephone and then walked off, as if her feelings had been hurt.

'It's me again,' he said. 'Is my dad still in Edinburgh?'

'Yes. He telephones twice a day. Conchita's such an anxious creature. She's not well too. We'll all have to be nice to her. You especially, Matthew. She talks a lot about you. She wants you to like her. She told me her birthday's next week, 8 April. It would be very kind of you if you were to send her a birthday card.'

But wouldn't he be a terrible hypocrite if he sent a card to someone he hated?

'We're going to cycle to Lochmaddy. There are shops there.'

'Take care.'

'There's not much traffic. Goodbye for now.'

'Goodbye.'

He went to look for Sheila and found her with the two

bicycles she had hired. She was cheerful. Her feelings hadn't been hurt. He didn't think they ever could be.

It took them over an hour to cycle to Lochmaddy. Sheila had now and then to wait for him; she kept getting in front.

'Why are you so slow?'

'This bicycle's too big for me.'

'That's not it. You're too slow. You're always slow. You're slow in everything.'

'Mrs Macdonald says it's because I think too much.'

'It's because you're just a child, that's why.'

Then she shot off again. leaving him far behind.

In Lochmaddy they looked round the shops. Matthew wanted to send a postcard to Mrs Macdonald. He chose one that showed the Caledonian McBrayne ferry from the mainland sailing into Lochmaddy; and there it was, the real thing, at the pier with its red funnels and attendant gulls.

They sat on rocks drinking lemonade and eating potato crisps and watching the people disembark. Passers-by gave them friendly glances, Sheila especially. It was as if it did them all good to see those two well-dressed, mannerly children, probably brother and sister, enjoying themselves so innocently in the sunshine with their bicycles beside them and gulls strolling round them in the hope of a share of the crisps.

Matthew had the postcard in his hand. 'What will I say on it?'

'Don't ask me.'

'Will I just say "Having a nice time"?'

'Very original.'

'Well, what would you say?'

'Nothing. Because I wouldn't send one.'

He felt provoked. 'I'm going to send another. Not a postcard, a birthday card.'

'I thought Mrs Macdonald's birthday was in November.'

'It's not Mrs Macdonald's.'

'Is it your father's?'

'No. It's hers.'

'You mean your stepmother's?'

'Yes. It's next week.'

He was sure she would laugh at him but no, she was enthusiastic. 'What a good idea! They'll never suspect you, when you kill her.'

'I'm not going to kill her. I told you I've changed my mind.'

'You're saying that because she's far away. When you get home and see her big stomach and stupid black face you'll hate her again.'

That was possible, so he said nothing.

Among the cards on display Sheila searched for one that applied to a stepmother. There was none. 'You'll just have to take one that says "mother".'

'She's not my mother.'

'Your father calls her your mother. I've heard him.'

'I'll never call her my mother.'

He might, though, in time call her his stepmother.

Every card had an affectionate greeting.

'If I sent it it would be a lie.'

'Don't you know, lies are necessary? People have to tell lies all the time. Stupid lies. This one wouldn't be stupid. It would please your father.'

He would do anything to please his father.

He chose a card that just said 'Happy Birthday'. He would write his name on it and nothing else.

They sat on a bench overlooking the pier. He wrote the address on the envelope. Sheila threw fragments of a scone to gulls.

'You know,' she said, 'I don't think your father would mind

very much if she was to die having the baby. He would be able to get on with his painting without being bothered. Lots of women die having babies. If you could manage to do something that would get rid of her and the baby at the same time it would be like killing two birds with one stone. You'd have your father to yourself then.'

He couldn't resist saying, 'He said if he went away again he'd take me with him.'

'There you are then.'

Thirty-Seven

Aunt Fiona met them at the door, holding Lucy in her arms.

'She jumped up on to my lap. She and I are going to be company for each other.'

Matthew was glad, though a little sad too.

Sheila sneered. 'Lucy knows it's your aunt that's going to feed her from now on.'

They had brought back scones and cakes for the tea.

'That was very kind of you,' said his aunt.

She's given in, he thought, she's already learnt to be humble.

He was still anxious to spare her feelings but Sheila said it didn't matter now.

He had noticed before how Sheila, after a period of being nice to everyone, suddenly got tired of doing it. She got edgy and forgot to smile. Usually she managed to correct herself at once and no one noticed, except him. He tried not to be alone with her when she was having one of these relapses.

Once, on the beach, she began to snatch up stones and hurl them at seals though they were well out of range. When he protested she threatened to throw them at him.

She screamed obscenities. 'I'm going to kill you, Matthew

Sowglass. And you know why. You're the only one who knows I killed Davy Moore. You'll give me away, you fucking little sneak, so I'll have to kill you before you do.'

Minutes later she was laughing at him for taking her seriously. The fit was over for now. He was in danger from her and he could see no escape.

On Sunday, to please Aunt Fiona, they attended a service in the Free Kirk church. Sheila quickly picked up the Gaelic responses and sang them as soulfully as any. Her piety was noticed. The worshippers, dressed in black, elderly, grim-visaged – smiling in the Lord's house was sinful – let Aunt Fiona know, by stern signs, that they were pleased with the girl, and with the boy too, though he had shown signs of restlessness towards the end: not, however, a grievous offence, for the service lasted nearly two hours and the wooden benches were unpadded.

When they got home he went into her room. She was lying on the bed, with her eyes closed. She was still wearing the black dress she had borrowed from Aunt Fiona.

'I want to say something,' he said.

'You needn't bother. I know what it is. I've been watching you. It's easy to tell what you're thinking. You've changed your mind. You don't want to kill your stepmother.'

He nodded.

'You're a liar, as well as a hypocrite. You still want her out of the way but you're too big a coward to do anything about it. That's it, isn't it?'

Yes, that was it.

Her eyes were still closed.

'Do you still pray for her to die?'

He did. He had done it in church.

'So what are you talking about? That's like killing her, isn't it? Only you want God to do it for you. But He won't, unless you help him. Now go away and leave me in peace.'

He went away but he didn't think he had left her in peace. She was never in peace, not even when she was asleep. He had once heard her wailing in her sleep, like an abandoned cat.

Thirty-Eight

When Miss Mairi McDougall, teacher in a primary school, and musical director of most of the local ceilidhs, heard that a guest of Miss McLure's had been proposed as a substitute for Mrs McPherson she groaned and hastened, in a state of anxiety, to put the girl to a test. The standard of singing and piano-playing might not be high but it had to be passable. In the past visitors who had volunteered had turned out to be tuneless screechers and key-thumpers. Miss McDougall had had to suffer several such excruciating experiences and she feared another, for any guest of Miss McLure was bound to be more pious than musical.

She was very pleasantly surprised therefore when, on calling at the cottage one evening, she met as attractive a girl as she had seen for a long time and, as a quick visit to the hotel piano proved, as accomplished a singer and pianist for her age as she had come across in years, and she was a regular attender at Mods, indeed was one of the judges. But what intrigued her most about Miss McLure's young guest was not her appearance or her talent but her enviable nature. Here was a charmer who not only had the ability to give pleasure but who enjoyed doing it. As she said to Miss McLure it was rare to find a child so lacking in conceit. It gave her an extraordinary quality of sincerity.

When he saw how captivated Miss McDougall was Matthew wasn't surprised. He knew music had that effect on Sheila. . . . In the house in Lunderston she would play the piano for hours at a stretch. 'She plays like an angel,' Mrs Macdonald would say, listening at the door; and, sure enough, when Sheila came into the kitchen, exhausted, she was so quiet and happy that he again doubted the gruesome stories she had told about herself and as for those occasions when he had actually seen her being bad, such as when she had lied about Davy Moore and when she had wantonly smashed the eggs, they could have been the consequence of a mental illness that affected her at some times. If that was so she deserved pity and help, not blame.

When he heard her singing or playing the piano, and when he saw how happy she was afterwards, he found himself feeling responsible for her, as if she really was his sister.

She came into his room to ask him, humbly, what songs she should sing at the ceilidh. He had heard her sing often, so he knew what songs suited her best. She didn't want to let his aunt down, or him, especially him. He knew, didn't he, that he was the person closest to her in the whole world. She had told him things she would never tell anyone else. She wasn't sure that he always believed her but it didn't matter. There was still something they had to do together. When it was done everything would be different.

It occurred to him that this would be a good time to ask her, more earnestly than ever before, if she really had killed Davy Moore, but he was afraid. She might say yes.

What was the something they had to do together. She had spoken as if it was unimportant, like washing the dishes, but it could be something terrible.

Would he advise her to sing 'Dream Angus', that nice little song about an old man who sold dreams to children, innocent dreams to innocent children? He had seen audiences spell-bound by her singing of that song.

210

'And the 'Fairy Lullaby?'

It was about a woman who left her baby while she went to gather blaeberries. When she came back her baby was gone. She searched everywhere but never found it. It had been stolen by fairies.

She would sing that song with great sadness.

Matthew couldn't help remembering the baby in the pram.

Miss McDougall approved of those two songs, especially as Sheila bravely offered to sing parts of them in Gaelic. Aunt Fiona would coach her.

Her third choice, though, puzzled Miss McDougall. It seemed to her inappropriate. Audiences, she pointed out, liked familiar songs; they could join in the choruses. Sheila said it had a connection with Uist, for it was about Bonnie Prince Charlie, who had once hidden on the island. Hadn't Flora Macdonald come from Uist?

Miss McDougall gave in.

As Matthew listened to Sheila practising that song he wondered if the 'bonny, bonny bird' that sang with such sorrowful passion was, in her mind, associated with the hedge-sparrow whose eggs she had so wantonly destroyed. Had she chosen those three songs because they had deep personal meanings for her, and were both a confession and an appeal?

Thirty-Nine

On the evening of the concert, when the people were arriving at the hotel and Sheila with the other performers were being given final instructions by Miss McDougall Matthew took the opportunity to telephone home.

To his delight it was his father who answered. He had just arrived home from Edinburgh, where, he said happily, his exhibition looked like being a success, but what pleased him more was the birthday card Matthew had sent to Conchita.

'We haven't given it to her yet. Tomorrow's her birthday. She'll appreciate it. It was very kind of you, Matthew.'

Matthew felt ashamed.

'How's Sheila?'

'She's singing at a ceilidh tonight.'

His father laughed. 'Good for her. She'll be singing at La Scala, Milan, one day.'

'What's that?'

'A famous opera house in Italy. What about you? Are you singing too?'

'No.'

'Well, I expect you'll want to say a few words to Mrs Macdonald.'

'Yes, please.'

It was always a relief to hear Mrs Macdonald's sensible voice.

'Hello, Matthew. Everything all right?'

'Yes, thank you. Sheila's singing at a ceilidh tonight.'

'She'll do well. She doesn't suffer from shyness, our Sheila. Did your father tell you your birthday card has arrived? In very good time. Her birthday's tomorrow. I'm glad you sent it.' Her voice dropped. 'She's a good soul, really. She's not well but she seems afraid to see a doctor. Your father's too concerned about his paintings. She doesn't complain. Poor soul. There was a big screed about your father in the *Scotsman*.'

'Did you cut it out?'

'Yes, I did. I knew you'd want to see it. It's very favourable. How is your aunt?'

'She's all right.'

But *was* Aunt Fiona all right? She had been very subdued lately. 'She's learning to be humble,' Sheila had said. But he thought he'd preferred her when she was proud.

'Have you sorted out that little difficulty about the money?'

'I think so.'

'Good. Trust Sheila.'

'I'll have to go now. The concert will be starting.'

'I wish I was there. But I'll sit in the kitchen and clap.'

He smiled. 'Good night.'

'Good night, Matthew. Take care. Everything's going to be all right.'

The big room where the ceilidh was being held was crowded. Aunt Fiona was keeping his seat for him at the front.

'Everything all right at home?'

'Yes, thank you. I was speaking to my dad. His exhibition in Edinburgh's a success.'

'I suppose that's all that matters.'

She immediately repented that bitter remark. 'I'm sorry. How is your stepmother, the Mexican woman?'

'She's not very well. Mrs Macdonald says she should see a doctor, but she doesn't want to.'

He remembered that Aunt Fiona refused to see a doctor about her sore back.

There were three performances before Sheila's: a fat woman sang a song in Gaelic that seemed to go on forever; a boy no older than Matthew played an accordion; and eight small girls sang in Gaelic. They were very neatly dressed in white blouses and tartan skirts. Matthew didn't think they were good at keeping in unison, but they were loudly applauded.

Then it was Sheila's turn. Matthew had had various emotions in relation to her but never before had he felt proud of her. He couldn't help it, she looked so distinguished. She was wearing a tartan skirt that Miss McDougall had borrowed for her. For someone like him who had seen her looking haughty and arrogant it was a wonder how she managed to look so meek and modest. Everyone in the room was pleased with her. Even if she sang indifferently they were ready to applaud her.

As soon as she began he knew that she wasn't singing merely to entertain these people, she was saying something about herself that, since they did not know her, they couldn't understand. He could, though, or thought he could.

The song 'Dream Angus', about the man who went about selling dreams, wholesome dreams, to children, was really a celebration of the innocence of childhood. As she sang it, with the necessary tenderness, Matthew remembered, as surely he was meant to, Davy Moore, whose head she had smashed in, or so she had boasted. Was she now, in this song, saying yes, she had done it and regretted it with all her heart, or was she telling him she hadn't done it at all, or could it be that she was saying she had done it and was glad?

She looked at him, noticed his perplexity, and smiled.

Not even he understood that smile.

When she was singing the next song, about the woman whose baby was stolen by fairies Matthew could not help remembering the baby in the pram whose horrible death she had caused, that was, if she had told him the truth. There was a verse in which the unhappy mother in her futile search saw 'the track of the swan upon the lake'. That was the one Sheila sang in Gaelic, passably so, judging from the appreciative applause.

To them she was simply a nice, talented girl singing a well-loved song very nicely.

When she sang the third song, though, with its passionate lament, some of the more imaginative ones felt a little uneasy. They knew, for Dugald the taxi-driver had spread the story, that her father had been drowned in a yachting accident not very long ago, and they felt that this intense grief could hardly be for a more or less mythical prince, but must be for her father.

In the second part of the concert she played on the piano a medley of Gaelic airs and then some pieces composed by herself. These were thought strange but brilliant.

All round him Matthew heard them murmuring that she had a glorious future either as a singer or a pianist. She was a very fortunate gifted girl.

Miss McDougall, though, when the people were skailing, came up to Matthew and Aunt Fiona. She was quite agitated. 'What an extraordinary performance! I hope she won't have to pay for it. I've never known a child her age show so much feeling. To tell you the truth it wasn't natural. Since both her parents are dead who looks after her?'

Matthew shook his head. No one looked after Sheila. She looked after herself.

'Much, much too intense,' muttered Miss McDougall. But then Sheila appeared, relaxed and happy.

Forty

Next morning, Saturday, 8 April, the brightness of the sun woke Matthew. Looking out of the window he saw the whole machair ablaze with light. Every blade of grass, every sheep's fleece, every bird in the sky, gleamed and glittered.

Today was his stepmother's birthday. He had begun to let himself think of her as his stepmother.

Then, out there in the midst of the splendour, a part of it with her shining hair, was Sheila. She seemed to be dancing. Her hands fluttered. She had a right to be happy after last night's triumph. Was she at last cured of whatever it was that was wrong with her?

Approaching the cottage, she caught sight of him at the window and waved. He waved back. This would be a good day for their exploration of the coast. He wouldn't be afraid of her. Hadn't she once said that he was the only person in the world that didn't disgust her?

He got up, washed, dressed, and went downstairs. Sheila was in the kitchen comforting Aunt Fiona. Yes, that was what she was doing. Aunt Fiona seemed to have been crying; she still was, though he couldn't see her face.

He didn't have to ask what was the matter. He knew. Aunt Fiona was lost. Not only had she had to learn to be humble, she had had to admit to herself that many of the things that she had been taught by her father weren't true. Among them was the belief that God had never intended people to be happy. She had condemned his mother for seeking happiness.

He went into the living-room where the table was set for breakfast.

Soon Sheila and Aunt Fiona brought in the porridge. Aunt Fiona smiled at him, but he was shocked by her appearance. He hadn't noticed before how thin her face had become, and how severe was the pain in her eyes.

Sheila chatted cheerfully. She was looking forward to walking along the shore as far as Saligo Bay, where, so the guidebook said, thousands of years ago there had been sacrifices to heathen gods. People had been put to death.

She asked Aunt Fiona if there were any children's spades and buckets in the cottage. Aunt Fiona said there were, Ailie Spence had left them. She added, with an attempt at humour, weren't Sheila and Matthew rather old to be building sand castles. 'Not the kind we're going to build,' said Sheila.

Matthew wondered what she meant.

Later in his room, while he was getting ready and making sure his compass was in his pocket, though it wouldn't be needed on so clear a day, Sheila came in.

'Today's your stepmother's birthday, isn't it?'

'Yes.'

'So it would be a good day to kill her.'

He supposed it was a joke but not one to laugh at.

'That's what you want, isn't it?'

No, it wasn't. He still wanted to get rid of his stepmother but he no longer wanted her dead.

'So that's what we'll do, kill her.'

How could they kill someone who was hundreds of miles away?

She in red jeans, he in blue, she carrying a child's spade, he a bucket, they set off. The picnic things were in a small rucksack on her back. He had binoculars slung round his neck.

At the door Aunt Fiona watched them until they disappeared among the dunes.

'She shouldn't be living alone,' said Sheila. 'She's lost confidence in herself. Haven't you noticed?'

He had but was surprised she had.

'Are you sorry for her?'

'Yes.'

'So why don't you come and live with her?'

He had let the thought pass through his mind.

'But of course once you've got rid of your stepmother you'll want to stay with your father.'

'Yes.'

'So let's get rid of her.'

Again he let it pass, though it worried him. What was she up to?

Keeping close to the sea they tramped across sandy bays and clambered over rocks slippery with seaweed. Once terns dived at their heads, protecting their nests, he thought. If he had seen any nests he wouldn't have told Sheila. Maybe she wasn't altogether cured.

They watched gannets plunge into the sea. He felt sorry for those who didn't come up with a fish.

They picked up shells off the sand. Among them were two unbroken sea-urchin shells.

They took their shoes off to walk across wet sand and put them on again to climb over rocks.

They came to a big depression in the sand, full of lukewarm sea water. Sheila proposed that they should have a swim.

He reminded her that they hadn't brought swimming costumes.

They didn't need them, she said.

Feebly he muttered that they didn't have towels.

The sun would dry them, she said.

To his horror she quickly stripped off all her clothes and, racing to the pool, dived in and began to swim. She was an expert swimmer, but it wasn't that he envied, it was her not being ashamed of being naked.

Anyone seeing them would have thought her the carefree one, he the one burdened with guilt.

She stood up in the pool. The water came up to her breasts. She was like a creature that had come out of the sea.

'Aren't you coming in?' she cried. 'It's lovely and warm. You won't drown. It's not deep.'

This was a situation where it was no advantage being one of the Chosen. No cloud obscured the sun, no rocks threw dark shadows.

Small crabs scuttled past his feet. They didn't have to be ashamed.

But he mustn't run the risk of destroying Sheila's carefree mood. So he undressed, but not completely: he kept on his underpants. Then he trudged to the pool and crept in. When he began to swim it was with a cautious breast-stroke. He twisted his neck, not to look at her, but to avoid looking at her.

The water was warm and pleasant but he soon discovered there were jelly fish in it. He couldn't tell if they were alive or dead but they were a good enough excuse for him to give up. 'Jelly fish!' he cried, and scampered back to his clothes. Though his underpants were soaked he put his jeans on over them, and his tee-shirt over his wet body.

Sheila kept swimming up and down the pool. She wasn't afraid of the jelly fish, but then she wasn't afraid of anything.

Surely she was the one protected by God. She, not him, was among the Chosen.

When at last she came out of the pool she danced about in the sun, getting dry. Drops of sea water sparkled on her body.

She sang a song he didn't know. Perhaps it was one she'd composed herself.

At last they came to the haunted bay. They recognised it by the six tall black stones in its midst and by the redness of the sand. This, according to legend, had been caused by blood. He did not feel like eating in such a place, but Sheila enjoyed the food Aunt Fiona had prepared for them: sandwiches with cheese and tomato, oatcakes, and apple pie.

They drank lemonade.

He was tired and sore from clambering over rocks and wanted to rest a while longer, but Sheila soon leapt up and walked towards the sacrificial stones, with the child's spade in her hand.

He followed slowly. He had put on his shoes, she was barefooted. His jeans were on properly, hers were rolled up to her knees. He had on his tee-shirt, she only her brassière.

It looked as if she was indeed going to build a sand castle.

'Aren't you going to help?' she cried. 'Are you afraid you'll get blood on your hands?'

All he would get on his hands was sand.

'What do you want me to do?'

'Build this heap higher. Use the bucket.'

Soon the heap was as tall as himself, but it wasn't until she fashioned a smaller heap into a ball as big as a head that he realised she was making a person, a crude one with no legs, like a snowman; or rather a snowwoman, for she was slapping lumps like breasts on to it.

It was meant to be his stepmother.

'Give me two small white shells.'

They were for eyes.

He took them out of his pocket. He touched his compass to protect him from Sheila's magic, whatever it was.

'Now find me some strands of black seaweed. There's plenty on those rocks.'

He found some and took it to her. She put it on the sandwoman's head, like hair. Then she drew a mouth with her finger.

She stood back and stared at it.

'It'll do. You know who it's meant to be, don't you?'

'No.'

'Yes, you do. It's your stepmother. There's just one thing to be done, the last thing. Do you know what this is?'

She took it out of her pocket.

'It's the shell of a razor fish,' she said.

He knew. He had seen fishermen dig razor fish out of the sand to use as bait.

The shell was about five inches long.

'But look, it's turned into a dagger. See.'

It was easy to see it as a dagger, the way she held it.

'You take it. It won't work if I do it. It's got to be you.'

'I don't want to.'

'Yes, you do. You want to get rid of her, don't you? Take it and stab her in the heart with it. You know where the heart is, don't you?'

All he would be doing was pushing an empty razor fish shell into a heap of sand.

'It's stupid.'

'It's not more stupid than praying for her to die. This is a kind of prayer. Didn't people hold services here?'

'Thousands of years ago.'

'But they're still here. Can't you see them? Can't you hear them?'

What he heard were the cries of birds, the slap of the waves, and his own heart beats.

Those heathens long ago must have heard the same sounds. But they had also heard the shrieks of the victim.

222

He decided to get it over with. He took the shell.

'Wait.' She looked at her wristwatch. 'What time do you make it?'

He looked at his watch. 'Three minutes to three.'

'Yes. Wait. Wait till it's exactly three.'

He waited. Those three minutes were a long time.

'Now,' she screamed. 'Now.'

He thrust the shell in and heard a shriek. It could have been Sheila, it could have been a sea bird, it could have been him.

He was going to pull the shell out and kick the sand until that was all it was, a heap of sand, but she stopped him.

'Let the tide do it. It will wash away all the blood.'

The tide was already flowing in. In a few minutes it would reach the effigy and destroy it.

Forty-One

Matthew was too tired to walk back, so they stood at the side of the public road waiting for a car to come along and give them a lift. Sheila was now respectably dressed and when a car came asked very politely. Luckily the driver and his wife, Mr and Mrs McFadyen, had been at the ceilidh and besides, knew Aunt Fiona well. They offered to take them to her cottage. They may have wondered what two children of twelve were doing so far from home with a spade and bucket more suitable for six-year-olds, but they were too mannerly to ask. When telling friends about the encounter they said they supposed that the girl had been trying to entertain the boy who was a shy wee fellow with little to say.

Aunt Fiona came to the door when the car arrived. She exchanged greetings in Gaelic with the McFadyens. Sheila thanked them again.

Somehow, said Mr McFadyen, in Gaelic, as they drove away, you wouldn't have expected a girl with her talents and advantages to be so modest and well mannered. Mrs McFadyen agreed.

Aunt Fiona had something to tell them, or rather to tell Matthew. It was so urgent she did it before they went into the house.

'There's been a message for you, Matthew. A boy came

from the hotel. You've to telephone Mrs Macdonald as soon as you can.'

'Did she say what it was about?'

'No. Will you go with Matthew, Sheila?'

He objected to being treated as if he was a child.

'We'll go on our bikes,' said Sheila. 'That's if you're not too tired. Do you want me to phone for you?'

He said he wasn't too tired. He was afraid something had happened to his father.

As they cycled along the track, trying to avoid the pot holes Sheila, ahead as usual, turned and shouted: 'What are looking so worried for? It's probably nothing. Mrs Macdonald's an old fusspot.'

At the hotel he made straight for the public telephone. He would have liked Sheila to go away and let his call be private, but she stayed close, eager to hear every word.

He listened to the ringing in the house in Lunderston. He felt homesick and anxious.

Then he heard Mrs Macdonald. 'Is that you, Matthew?'

'Yes, it's me. Is there something wrong?'

'I'm afraid there is.'

'It's not my dad, is it?'

'No, it's not him. It's your stepmother. She's just been taken to hospital.'

He felt great relief, not because the woman was ill but because it wasn't his father. 'What's the matter with her?'

'It seems she's had a heart attack.'

'Ask her what time it happened?' whispered Sheila.

'When did it happen?'

'The exact time, ask her the exact time.'

'About two, two hours ago.'

'It couldn't have been. She's making a mistake. It was three o'clock.'

'Is that Sheila with you?'

225

'Yes.'

'That's good. She's a sensible girl. She'll look after you.'

'I don't need her to look after me.'

'No, of course you don't.'

'Is she dead? Ask her if she's dead.'

'Is she dead?'

Mrs Macdonald was shocked. 'Of course she isn't. It wasn't a very severe attack.'

'She's just saying that. She doesn't want to frighten you. Ask her about the baby. Is it dead too?'

'Is the baby all right?'

Mrs Macdonald was touched. 'Yes, thank goodness.'

'She's lying.'

'Sheila seems to be doing a lot of whispering.'

'Yes. Is my dad all right?'

'He's fine. He's very worried of course. He's at the hospital now.'

'Does he want me to come home?'

They were due to return in four days.

'I don't think that's necessary. Finish your holiday. She's not in danger.' Mrs Macdonald hesitated. 'I ken, son, you weren't very pleased that she'd come, you wanted your father to yourself, but she's really a good soul, and she was terribly pleased with the card you sent her. You've not to think of her as trying to take your mother's place. She knows she could never do that, but I'm sure you could come to be fond of her.'

He shook his head, but he knew that it could happen. He never bore grudges long. He didn't know his stepmother. It was possible she could become his friend, like Mrs Macdonald. It wasn't her fault she was allergic to cats.

'By the way,' said Mrs Macdonald, 'there's another bit of news that will interest you. They've got the man that killed wee Davy Moore.'

He looked at Sheila. 'Did you hear that?'

She had heard it. She looked as if she was going to cry. She was like a little girl who had been found out. She reminded him of Ailie Spence.

'It's a lie,' she said, and rushed away.

So it had all been lies. But why had she needed to tell them?

'It seems he's from Gantock. It's in all the newspapers.'

'Aunt Fiona doesn't get a newspaper.'

'Well, it's front-page news. It's a great weight off everybody's mind. We didn't like to think it was somebody from Lunderston. Give my regards to Sheila and your aunt. Give Lucy a pat for me.'

'Yes, I will. Please give mine to my dad and' – he hesitated – 'to my stepmother. I hope she gets better soon.'

'I'll do that, son, gladly. See you soon. God bless you.'

Mrs Macdonald was crying.

There were tears in his own eyes.

He wouldn't know what to say to Sheila.

Epilogue: Twenty Years Later

O ne sunny June morning three of Lunderston's superior matrons, hair blue-rinsed and accents carefully pruned of vulgar Scotticisms, were enjoying their usual coffee and chocolate biscuits at a window table in Black's upstairs tea-room, with a good view of the main street below. It wasn't the baskets of flowers, mainly geraniums, hanging from the lamp-posts, or the immaculacy of the pavements, or the smartness of the various shops, that interested them, though of course they approved of these; it was the variety of people. In their hearts they knew that what they were doing, gossiping like sweetie wives, was as vulgar as saying didnae instead of didn't or sma' instead of small, but they didn't feel penitent. After all they had been born in the town, had had their children in its hospital (now, alas, closed) worshipped in it (they had the choice of two Church of Scotland kirks, St Cuthbert's or St Margaret's) and probably would be buried in it, though the old kirkyards were almost full. So, to use a word hardly ever spoken aloud, they loved it and wished it well. Some of their comments might have been construed by a stranger as being somewhat censorious, but Lunderstonians would have de-tected the disguised goodwill.

Two persons particularly interested them, a middle-aged woman and a young man, who were chatting outside Stra-

chan's electric goods shop. The former looked, and no doubt
sounded, common. If they had encountered her in the street
by herself they would have passed without so much as a nod.
Yet they knew quite a lot about her. Her name was Moore.
She lived in a council flat in the Glebe, a run-down housing
scheme. She spoke working-class Scots shamelessly. Ordinary
in every other way she had a terrible distinction. Twenty years
ago her son Davy, aged ten, had been murdered.

But it was the young man they were eager to talk about. He
was well dressed, in a dark business suit. Though bareheaded
he gave the impression of often wearing a hat and of doffing it
to women.

'What on earth can they have to talk about?'

'He knew her boy.'

'I believe he was in the same class at school.'

'It was more than that. He was at the funeral.'

'Heavens, practically the whole town was at that funeral. I
was there myself. That awful Orange band.'

'But he was there as an invited guest. He was in the
limousine beside her. I saw him myself.'

'So did I. His father was abroad at the time.'

'You know, they never got anyone for the murder.'

'They thought they had but it was a mistake.'

'So it's possible a murderer's been walking loose in the town
for the past twenty years.'

'It makes you shiver to think about it.'

'It's funny Sowglass having so little ambition. You'd have
thought he would have made use of his university degree.'

'What use could he have made of it? It was for some silly
subject. Philosophy, I think.'

'Are you saying philosophy's silly?'

'You know what I mean. It's useless, as far as getting you a
good job.'

'Isn't running the Gallery a good job?'

The Gallery sold paintings and objets d'art, all exquisite and expensive. Its customers came from far and wide. Young Sowglass was reputed to be an expert. Which was no wonder really, considering that his father, Hugh, was a famous artist who lived in Paris. One of his paintings was in the window of the Gallery, for show, not for sale. Not that anyone in the town could have afforded it. Even Hugh Sowglass's smallest paintings cost thousands, and this, a whirlwind of violent colours, was large.

'Why has our Matthew never got married? Do you think he's one of those?'

That was a naughty little joke. They licked chocolate off their lips and smiled.

'We know why he's not attracted to our Lunderston girls, don't we?'

Yes, they knew, but still they asked, 'Do we?' still smiling. 'Tell us.'

'In two words, Sheila Burnside.'

'Ah yes, Sheila Burnside.'

Though she had been born in Glasgow, Lunderston claimed Sheila as one of them. Even those townsfolk who couldn't stand opera, and they were many, were proud of her, already at thirty-two an internationally famous soprano, noted for the thrilling quality of her singing of passionate arias. She was also supremely beautiful.

'They were very close at one time, weren't they?'

'She lived with him when they were children. Mrs Macdonald looked after them.'

'After her father died in the yachting accident.'

'They spent holidays together in the Hebrides, with his aunt.'

'She was staying with him when that ghastly accident happened to the woman his father brought back from South America.'

'From Mexico, I think.'

'She fell downstairs, didn't she, and was killed?'

'She was pregnant at the time, wasn't she?'

'The child died too.'

'You couldn't say Matthew's been lucky.'

'No. His father went off again.'

There was a pause.

'To get back to Sheila, wasn't there talk of her marrying a wealthy Italian, a count or something?'

'It came to nothing.'

'Maybe because it's our Matthew she's interested in.'

'If she is goodness knows why.'

But they knew a reason, though they would never have mentioned it. Matthew Sowglass had a quality that they would have been embarrassed to give a name to, at any rate aloud. It was goodness, of a kind so genuine as to be inoffensive.

'Aren't we forgetting Veronica?'

Though that was said with an attempted twinkle, and though they all laughed, they were obviously uneasy. They had daughters of their own. If Matthew Sowglass hadn't taken Veronica Hamilton into his house, she would have rotted away in a mental institution. Come to think of it his was a household of rather odd women: his gaunt aunt who had come from the Hebrides to be his housekeeper; Bella Macdonald, his ex-housekeeper, now over eighty; and poor daft Veronica.

Had nature been trying to compensate by making Veronica so good-looking, not in the way film stars were good-looking, and Sheila Burnside for that matter, but as female saints in holy pictures were? If that had been nature's intention it had been a mistake. There was that awful blankness in her eyes. It was said that the only time it vanished, and then only for seconds, was when she was looking at Matthew Sowglass.

There was of course nothing between them. You would have to be a very bad-minded person indeed to think so.

Leaving tips on the table, the three ladies went downstairs, through the baker's shop with its delectable smells, and out into the bright street.

They were in time to see Matthew Sowglass walking towards the Gallery.